ANSAKI DEVOUT

Paul OGarra

Dedication

To the sacred memory of the tens of thousands of children of Palestine murdered vilely and brutally by World leaders in quest of personal gain, and in full knowledge of the fact that they were assassinating little children.

In the sure belief that the Good Lord holds their unblemished souls in eternal rest.

To all those worthy people who preserve our values as moral human beings, often to the detriment of their careers, jobs, livelihoods, and the loss of their lives. In the face of a new breed of evil international criminals who bask in the tranquility of, and constantly abuse a security humanity has fought for, and attained over the centuries.

To my mother and father who taught me what love is, and about God.

Contents

Chapter One:
Benahavís

I was shown to my seat by a smart-looking girl, an usherette, sporting a stylish corporate uniform. The venue was this upmarket conference hotel in a spa town in the hills behind Marbella with a river flowing through. I parked the bike right by the entrance steps, just so I could keep an eye on it.

"Witches and Naturopathy conference hang-out. Is this it?" They looked at me quizzically from behind their reception desk. I must have looked gormless to them, standing there dressed in my usual Nepalese hippie trousers, the bright yellow ones with floating stars and stuff. They stared at me in the way only *casposos* (poseurs, I suppose) of the Costa Del Sol can master, a sort of *"Aver este tio* (will you look at this goon), *Jaja,"* a hidden look, a mute smile between them, *"Guiri?"* (northern European or English, a derogatory term) again unspoken. More of them converged on me from around the gaping lobby until I was surrounded by their all- matching corporate gear, the same colour for boys and girls. I raised my voice an octave or two or six, as no one seemed to be answering.

"Is it or isn't it, *Pichita?"* Using the local dialect immediately dispels the idea that the subject is an uninformed foreigner. *Pichita* means "little willie" in Cadiz lingo, an affectionate term as all things Cadiz, or *Gaditano*. Well, the *pichita* could here be interpreted as a challenge to their unashamed *caspoteo*.

But I followed up with a claim to fame to which I was not entitled. "It's me, Rico, the King of Hemp – *el Rey del Cáñamo*," using both languages just to throw them off balance. Lavishly, with wide gestures, I then produced my invite, very crumpled from my bike ride but bearing the impressive name and title Dr Alarico O'Donovan de Medinacheli. Well, they got all flustered and started calling me Doctor and Sir, and then this Top Usherette, who they must have summoned, came clicking her way over and carried me off to my appointed cloud to await the show.

"Are you really the King of Hemp?" she enquired with a big smile.

"Naw, of course, I'm not, but I went to school with him, I've visited his cave and been arrested with him once, but they all believed it," I said, and I began laughing and she started giggling and one of her girlfriend usherettes came over and got giggling as well, and people started looking. There were hundreds of them at this big do in this incredibly posh hotel called Villa Something or Other, and my invite was real.

"After the show, we'll all go to one of my fields and have a laugh," I said lightly. "You can bring everyone. They'll all get shitfaced just from the smell."

They looked at me agreeing and wondering. They must have been hallucinating about how I thought this conference of really straight-looking business people would follow me on my motorbike with my screaming

2

yellow pants, Free Julian Assange face mask, and Palestine T- shirt. Well, to tell the truth, I was quite mortified to see the turnout here this evening. I had been expecting a bunch of switched-on people into an alternative style of business and life.

"They're not your sort," she said.

"It's just the clothes," I replied with a grin. She was growing on me by the minute. "How about if I strip? Then we'll all be cool."

"Nonononono," she stuttered as I started pushing down my yellow pants. So, I yanked them back up.

"Later then," I said with a wink. "It's a date." So, she smilingly pushed me backward into my seat and marched off.

I looked around hoping to find some herbal types, someone like the many older locals I had met over the years in and around the country towns behind the Costa, Coin, and Alhaurin, who used to collect their own herbs, their manzanillas and jaras. One old boy from Coin, *El Chumpero* as they used to call him; he was a *curandero*, a healer, who used to collect herbs and service many people with his *Uñas de gato. Ortigas salvajes* and all sorts. My father used to talk about going out into the countryside with him on the night of St John, the summer solstice. This was the time of the year that had the most light and was ideal for the collection of medicinal plants. The days are longer and the sunlight is transformed into the lifeblood, the principal ingredients of the plants, and as a consequence enhancing their healing properties.

My father and uncle once found a sack made of a hessian-type material up the chimney, on a hidden ledge, of a ruined cottage in the Alozaina area. They had found a golden sweet *manzanilla*, camomile. Inside the sack was a rough piece of card identifying the contents as having been collected *En el menguante de San Juan en el año Del Señor 1930*. That meant it was collected during the waning of the moon, on the night of St John in the year of Our Lord 1930. This rich treasure had lain there even during the murderous years of the bloody Spanish Civil War. Rich, because my father would make us all tea with it adding the honey that one of the friends of El Chumpero had sold him many years before. Well, my father said that the night of St John was a magical night. He and the old man would collect herbs, and the old woman would prepare a cauldron, set it over a bonfire, and when the men returned, they would cast the herbs into the boiling broth.

In later years, when I appeared on the scene and as I grew, my life was always tinged with the wonder of it all, the magic. I came to understand the enchantment of this night, the night of Janot, of witches, of St John. The night in which the doors of both kingdoms lay open, the divide between the physical realm and that of the spirits.

The conference began, and I soon realised that it was not a gathering for people involved with Witches and Naturopathy at all, it was just a giant Tupperware-style get-together to promote different lines of vitamins and patented herbal remedies. I remembered the trouble I had had to get seeds of the devil's claw, a natural and wondrous anti-inflammatory that grew wild in the Namibian desert and had been used medically by the natives for thousands of years. I wanted to cultivate a field of it and make it freely available to all the older generation and their arthritis, but try as I might it seemed impossible to find seeds. So many species had started to go missing.

It was a total mystery until I learned of the sterilisation programmes for plants being carried out by various multinationals. They had done it with the staple foods, wheat, barley, corn, and the rest. They created a genetically modified strain and introduced it to poor farmers in Pakistan and India. The wonderful new version was readily available and at giveaway prices. Through a whole army of salespeople and the cooperation of an unsuspecting (or corrupt) ministry, the new wondrous staple food seeds were introduced. The fruit of the new plants was magnificent, and sales soared. The farmers were delighted, and abandoned their careful husbanding of seedlings from harvest to harvest, to rely exclusively on the new genetically modified seeds. All was rosy in the garden.

And then the prices soared, and many farmers were made bankrupt. Some hanged themselves. Then to make matters worse, seed laws were introduced and the world's food supply slowly fell under the dominance of dubious multinationals. I hadn't realised that there were multinational companies involved in agriculture, and then it hit me – there were the Ba..., the Co..., the ChemC..., the Limag..., and others. No longer could farmers plant the seeds they preferred. This sort of insidious takeover started to spread to anything that grew and was consumed by humanity. They wanted to control it all, everything.

And here I was stuck on the front row of a gathering of would-be distributors of vitamins and other packaged natural products. At a break in the presentation, I leapt onto the stage. Thankfully it wasn't very high.

"I am the King of Hemp," I shouted. They must have decided to humour me as part of the show, as a light came to bear on me and a hanging mike suddenly hovered overhead. They probably thought it would be better than a streaker. The public must have been bored to tears as I just bowed around a bit and they started clapping.

"The magical night of St John and its rituals involve the use of those holy or sacred herbs which nature gives us so freely, and which are a wonderful source for remedies and cures. *Hypericum perforatum*," I shouted, waving my arms for effect, and they clapped. "Verbena *and Salvia officinalis*," I screamed, they shouted, and the organisers started a musical drumbeat through the speakers to add to the happening. "Artemisa, Achillea, Ruscus," I chanted, and they repeated it.

Then I raised my two hands palms out to stop them. Suddenly there was silence. I could see most of the faces, just sitting there. They were in Spain, it was a break for them, they were getting treated to a free holiday so they could return to their own places of origin and help to sell the product being produced by a pyramid at the top of which sat some corrupt multinational that had stolen nature's product, sterilised it and made it their own. That product would never again regenerate itself as nature had designed; only the multinational now had the power to do that, and all for money, for profit, for power. I got carried away and said lots of this to the people gathered until I could see that security people were heading my way.

"These people are killing, sterilising our plant world. They are evil and must be stopped," I shouted. A couple of very large hotel security people came over. I ran from them shouting, "Grow your own, don't buy their poison." Then a motley crew of very aggressive women and a few large men descended on me, and I ran.

It was a shame. I would have rather liked to chat to that usherette, to have a laugh at everything that had gone down. So I drove around the town to kill time till the show ended. It was a helluv'an incredible place. I drove right up to where the river came charging down, hitting rocks and meandering slightly. Here the Angosturas Gorge with its long canyons and multiple rock pools and rockslides provided adventure for the thousands of kids of the area who spent their summer afternoons canyoning and enjoying its delights.

I wanted to see the usherette so I could josh her about what had happened, and we could laugh and make a huge joke about it. But I was hurting, hurting bad. It had been a reminder of all that was going on around the planet. The kids in Palestine weren't messing about having fun and adventure in water and rock pools and beaches, they were being daily set upon by Israeli settler bullies or troops, kidnapped and left to languish in military prisons, evicted from their homes complete with their extended families, bombed indiscriminately, fenced in and deprived of supplies, medicines, and being shot out of hand if they dared to raise a voice in protest. Friends the world over would send me photos, or I would read it up on Twitter or Facebook or free press outlets such as C...punch. It was going on daily. In Yemen, hundreds of thousands of kids were starving to death. Rogue bombers from Saudi and the UAE, backed by the US and Canada, were dropping US bombs, all in the name of profit, on the city of Sanaa. And there were so many issues everywhere about everything. The little man was getting screwed left right and Centre while the super-rich were getting away with murder.

And the reason for so many conferences and so many US businesses suddenly showing a massive interest in southern Spain was because of a US politician, one of the really dodgy ones. A prime mover in the energy industry and CEO of those very agricultural multinationals waging war on the plants of the world. The same man, a senator, headed all sorts of committees to protect the environment, did the same in the world of energy, and was a strong member of the pro-Israel lobby. Israel was receiving 3.8 billion US dollars per annum to finance her war against the poor destroyed Palestine people, a people who were suffering and nailed to the ground. Yes sir, this guy was rotten. How can you own massive oil companies and be on government boards created specifically to limit their power, and support Israel's war on the innocent people of Palestine, their cousins? Well, this same man, complete with his family and, I imagine, a massive entourage was visiting us here on the Costa Del Sol.

I had spent my youth tweeting away, carrying billboards, and wearing T-shirts, and it was a battle against a volcano that spewed into every nook and cranny before you could even begin to think about countering its power. These guys were just evil, but they were human beings and they could be stopped. Regardless of how many things they managed to get into, how many wars they started, people they killed, and how much money they stole and power they assimilated, they could always be stopped and a groundswell created against them. It would just take lots of guts and perseverance.

ANSAKI DEVOUT

Chapter Two:
Delaisandra

I lay partially in the sun, the rest of me hidden away under a big, heavily draped beach umbrella. I was thinking about boys and men, and how, even now, they had not the scantiest idea of what a girl was about. And to crown it all, our multiple sexualities, as females, were of late legal and smiled upon, so that they, the men's, knowledge of who we actually were had become more obscure than ever.

It wasn't interest, just curiosity. I had lost interest long before men and boys had started to bore me. It seemed that whilst women appeared to develop stronger and more interesting psyches, the male side seemed to have shrivelled up.

A person with no aura, no mind, no something special, and I certainly don't mean anything physical, was fast becoming a non-person, a sort of zombie for me. What door to lay the blame at? A bit of a quandary, but people were fast becoming so "the same" that at times, because of a lack of real people to mix with, one could believe one's sanity was threatened.

I must confess that I did have a short period of messing with social media, Twitter in particular. The Word that sprang to mind was "sponge" – all it achieved was to give me the occasional bout of depression, a condition whose existence I had always denied, and to suck away my hours uselessly writing messages that no one would ever read, simply because the other tweeters were all too busy writing their own tweets, or retweeting inane articles that thankfully – I say thankfully because apart from a few talents, the journalistic content left much to be desired – I never got to read. It had become a world of tweeting twits.

And on the occasions that one wandered out into the real world, it was full of zombified consumers on holiday, attempting unsuccessfully to rid themselves of long-accumulated stress, so that when I wasn't in the hills watering my grandfather's infant Jamun trees, I would escape to this beach club, ignore the snobbery of my fellow patrons and just lie back and read a good book.

The waiters and beach attendants, be they male or anything else, fawned over me simply because I looked like someone who could be someone, or with someone. Marbella and its mirages were just down the road, and the glitterati reputedly came in search of the glitterati, when in fact the true haut monde escaped at a gallop from all such vulgarities. Of course, I had a hell of a sweet behind, the narrow-hipped long-type, and a beautiful cherubic face which during my narcissistic moments I fell deeply in love with myself. Thankfully such moments were rare, which was fine as I decidedly despised the selfie breed we had created with our gimmicky hi-tech. It so happened that today was one of those rare days when I truly felt incredible. I had languished before the mirrors in the palatial changing rooms for half the morning before venturing out to the envious glances of the paltry competition. That's not me at all, I am not a competitor, but it seemed that my enchantment was improperly playing with my hormones.

"May I get you something?"

I just turned my face toward her. One of the others had sent her over for a peek. She blushed, quite becomingly. My startling blue eyes often have that effect. She was young, probably in her teens. I teased her.

"What would you have for me?" I had opened the door to all sorts of possible quips or remarks, perhaps hoping for a witty natural for which Cadiz was famous, although Malaga also had its fair share. I was disappointed though, she had nothing to offer me, only her pretty little blush and cute teen body and face, none of which were of interest to me. Then surprisingly she blushed bright again. I glanced around.

He hauled himself out of the water onto the wooden jetty boards, dripping glittering sundrops. I could feel him, his presence, and even though his eyes roved over in my general direction he didn't see me. I was just part of the landscape. He must have measured well over six and a half feet and even though he was not young, probably in his late fifties, sported an immensely powerful torso and arms. I knew what an enigma he was – after all, the human body was essentially my domain. Swimmer's muscles, rippling, no gym artificiality. He wore a full-body swimsuit, blue and yellow. I had never seen a specimen like him; he was truly magnificent. But he was scarred in many places, those I could see. They had tried to plastic it away, but there was just too much, probably knife wounds and bullet holes. Naked it would have been, presumably, a complete tapestry – and tattoos of all colours and hues, the story of a violent human life.

The attendants ran up to him with towels, and as he dried off and they spoke to him, he in turn patted both of them, young boys, on their heads in a wonderful paternal sort of way. They looked at him and spoke smilingly, intimately, trying so obviously to ingratiate themselves with him, in a manner that spoke volumes about this charismatic individual. And his face, the face of an Atilla the Hun, smooth in an Asiatic way, yet again they had not had enough artistry to magic away the ravages of his life, whatever they may have been. Savage yet beautiful.

I suppose I am painting a rather pathetic picture of myself as I enter this narrative. I should effect an introduction, for no other reason than to account for my activities, aptitudes, and skills which may otherwise throw the story into some sort of tailspin and eventual confusion.

I was born in Cuba twenty-seven years ago. My grandfather was a civil engineer, who the economic blockade of the country had forced to take on employment outside his profession, often as a waiter, a disc jockey, or whatever he was able to find. After wasting part of his life (although he, being a greatly philosophical person, merely considered it positive drifting), he did indeed get involved in many fascinating jobs, ranging from a few years as a *Santero* holding "Toques de Santo", the traditional ritual in which an *Oricha*, a sort of saint, was called down to possess one of their faithful, to skippering a racing trimaran. That career ended dismally when he and another crew member fell off the craft some eight kilometres off Varadero and had to swim to land, suffering the bad luck of running into a shoal of Portuguese Man of War jellyfish, which left them weeping and shouting in pain until a passing fishing boat rescued them and the seamen applied fresh urine and vinegar to their stings.

He finally managed to secure a proper job as an engineer in Spain, and we left, my grandmother, my mother who was only sixteen, and baby me. They named me Delaisandra, a typical Cuban custom of combining names, in this case, Delilah and Delisandra (protectress of the earth). My mother was fair of complexion and had fallen in love with a Cuban beach bum, a diver who used rocks as weights to take him down into the murky depths till he, I am told, punctured a lung and disappeared from my life.

I was a natural athlete and shone in my studies, as so many marginalised immigrants tended to do if they had the brains. I did political sciences at UCL and then went on to finish a degree in journalism. I got a few writing jobs, but soon realised that the industry was being trashed, like most professions, by mighty companies, so using my few, and grandfather's many, contacts and friends I began to freelance, getting my foot in the door slowly with good, solid, well- investigated articles.

I saw the big guy again in the dining section of the club. He was unobtrusively seated in a far corner of the room behind a screen. I only spotted him because I was looking out for a girlfriend I had made a lunch date with. He wasn't alone, and as I craned my neck around the screen for a discreet look, three faces met my enquiring gaze with unveiled hostility, to which I rapidly interjected, "Sorry, just looking for a friend."

He, the big man, a fourth face, did not look hostile; he just looked at me, the glimmer of a smile showing at the corners of his mouth. Then they looked away and went back to their conversation in what I thought at the time was some sort of Arabic, but later learned was Pashto, interspersed with Ossetic, Urdu, and apparently smatterings of Russian. My trained and nosy journalist's mind immediately started trying to fathom out who his friends were, and who he was himself for that matter.

Then a waiter came up to advise me that my friend had arrived. The daughter of a large, prosperous family from Seville, Rocio – an incredible Spanish name meaning Dew – had, by virtue of a longstanding childhood connection, an in with the top echelons of the Cadiz Guardia Civil. Her connection was with the commanding general of the zone, so she was virtually a VIP in any of the *comandancias* such as Cadiz or Malaga, which were run by a colonel or lieutenant colonel.

Spain, as you may be starting to imagine, is a tremendously nepotistic setup. The fact of the matter is that even large foreign multinationals operating within Spain are invariably swept up by her nepotistic charms and end up selecting staff much along such lines in order to survive. Spain's nepotism is essentially part of her culture, all political opinions practise it, and it seems impossible that it will ever be eradicated.

We got to chatting, and for a while, any thoughts of the big man and his dinner companions went completely out of my head. Rocio was also a journalist. She was older than I, in her forties, probably gay, in fact definitely not heterosexual, so I decided not to gossip about the lovely-looking big mysterious man who had climbed out of the sea.

The conversation was all about her and her latest project, an attack on Spanish plutocracy.

"Spanish?" I retorted, "At least here we're fighting back. You need to go to the USA. It's a real shit – their politics are so bipolar that the rich not only rule, the playing field is so tilted against the common man and woman that the rich are practically unassailable. They say that two percent of the population of the USA is as wealthy as all the rest of the country."

"It's the same plutocracy as ours. The US is successfully exporting it all over." "Was, is, Grump a plutocrat?"

"A buffoon, a wannabe. Could have done so much. Remember the main wealth is often not visible. Who knows, people like Beton, and Zuckerbee, may well not even be their own men. They may be puppets."

"Yeah, I remember when the rich and powerful were quite shy about publicity. Perhaps the real people, the families behind the power and wealth of the world, are people we have never even heard of. My grandfather used to remark about the Lindbergh kidnapping, that it was probably when the wealthy started to run scared."

"I think it was Bonaparte who said something about the poor allowing the rich to be rich because of religion."

"Here it is on the internet," I said. "Napoleon: 'There must be religion, otherwise the poor would murder the rich.'"

"Well, he got it arse about face. It's the rich who are doing the murdering, by proxy, through armies, drones, and bombing. Who knows? it may just be a temporary phase."

"A temporary phase in what?"

"In the growing up of the democratic child. Democracy is still a baby, still growing. Who knows, the next phase may well be Bonaparte hitting the nail on the head. The religionless populace may start assassinating the very rich."

"They'd certainly have it coming. Consider that once upon a time it was deemed wise to allow the middle classes to survive, in a subservient sort of way, and the working classes to live well. But today the rich are so obsessed that the lowly are at odds to make ends meet, and often not only the lowly. The old conception that anyone from any level of society could become a billionaire has worn thin over the last decade. Do you as a middle-class Spaniard not fear the possible onset of a new civil war or some sort of civil strife in the near future?"

"No, not at all," Rocio replied. "Well, at the worst some half-cocked affair by the so-called extreme right. No, the danger lies in places like India, with Modi and his Bharatiya Janata Party. It appears that they are gearing up their armoury to do battle against their own people. But there is always the possibility of China or someone else financing the creation of a people's army strong enough not just to bloody Modi's nose, but topple the government and establishment of the country.

"And what is it about? Just the farm deal, the turning the Indian farms over to the corporations?"

"It's about everything, wanting to steal the whole country for themselves. Personally, I think it's a very stupid philosophy. At some juncture, things will start to give, how exactly I don't know, but I am convinced that our current Western leaders have little or no idea of the way forward.

As we left the beach club, emerging onto the carpark to feel the still-hot afternoon sun, we could hear the cicadas rattling away, singing their song of love and repelling every predatory bird for miles around. The sound of motorbikes revving up made us turn and look. I recognised the Farsi speakers despite their helmets, all riding top-of-the-range bikes which glistened aggressively in the brilliant sunlight. I recognised them because I was looking intently, subconsciously searching for him. And then he also drove past with a smile and a small wave or salute of sorts. He also rode a big bike, but it was vintage and stylish, and it needed to be big because he was a big, very big, man.

Chapter Three:
The Senator

A murmur of voices hangs in the heat of the Andalusian evening. The sky is still glaringly blue, and the sun is travelling timelessly in the direction of what, it being August, is still some degrees south of due west. A slight breeze brings relief and gives rise to a barely perceptible rustle in the small forests of pine and eucalyptus that surround the Polo Club. One can discern the proximity of the Mediterranean and its tan lotion-soaked beaches by the gradual approach of a vague sea mist that tastes faintly of salt.

A buzz, a loud murmur is created by the crowds. Part of it yet set apart is the metallic sound of a commentator enunciating clearly but rapidly and excitedly. There are contributions in what appears to be Argentinian Spanish, a quite understandable variant of the original European language, punctuated with everyday Argentinian expressions such as *vistes* and *pelotudos*. Interviews are conducted with various experts and horse breeders and an American, probably a Texan. The accent of the interviewee is very JR, no mistaking.

Sotogrande's polo academy is huge and attracts the children of the rich from all over the world. Visitors have included sheiks from the Gulf states and the British royal family. During the event, which goes on for some five weeks, the three pistes each host a game in which the jockeys, wearing their team colours with regulation helmets and knee guards, slice at the ball, which is nowadays made of high-impact plastic. Named the Argentinean ball, it has of late replaced the bamboo version. When British officers stationed just across the frontier in Gibraltar first practised the sport here, they used a white-painted, leather-covered cricket ball.

The mist continues on its landward journey and slowly begins to encroach on the pistes. The exclusive Sotogrande development was constructed in 1964 by an American-Filipino businessman called McMicking, on a beachside plot of 1800 hectares of land known as Finca Paniagua. It was the first act in the destruction of one of the most beautiful beachfronts in the world, the Costa Del Sol. The mist has always invaded the low-lying land that runs for some three kilometres inland and is today again reclaiming part of the estuary of the River Guadiaro and those undulating, incredible beaches that were once home only to the local fisherfolk and fauna.

A motorcycle of the type used to navigate rough countryside terrain has entered a field directly facing the VIP building next to the central polo piste, but outside the fences surrounding the complex. The rider clambers off and unstraps a surfboard from the side of the bike. It fits so snugly that it seems to belong there. He leans the board, which is tightly fitted into a white cloth bag, against the bike and checks the controls on a large hydraulic machine standing next to a clump of trees. He works as slowly and methodically as any Andalucian worker in the heat of an

August afternoon. The key is in the ignition, and he starts the motor, which is surprisingly silent-running. The machine, a hydraulic elevator, looks quite new. He leaves it running and unbags the surfboard. From a large section cut out of the board, he takes a rifle body, and then the telescopic sights which are stored separately. He is clearly experienced in the assembly and arming of the weapon, as it is ready to fire within seconds. He hits the hydraulic lift control, and it starts to raise him toward the tree line.

A massive force of uniformed police and Guardia Civil patrols the VIP leisure section between the pistes. The Guardia Civil, popularly named "La Benemerita", is a paramilitary force formed in 1844, whose history in the defence of the freedoms and the people of the country culminated nearly a hundred years later when eighty-three percent of the Guardias who fell in the Spanish Civil War did so in defence of the Republic. When the rebels under Franco won the war with outside help, the Guardia Civil was reorganised; with the onset of democracy and modernity, it was reformed once again, welding it into an efficient modern police entity.

There are men in black suits and dark sunglasses everywhere, a bit like a Matrix movie. The entrance gates are densely controlled by uniforms and black suits, all vying for size although the black suits seem to have it; enormous men, but slim and fit. There's a big crowd of visitors, thousands, with hundreds more lining up at the access point.

The presence of so much security is due to the visit of an American senator, an extremely powerful and pivotal man in the ruling party. Helicopters are overflying the zone and two enormous vans sprouting a host of antennae are likely to be the control centres for the myriad drones also hovering over the area. So much is in the air it's surprising they don't collide. Much of the space in the vast carparks is occupied by a regiment of official cars and police and Guardia carriers of all descriptions. As the afternoon progresses, the sea mist brings an air of mystery and a tendency to distort sounds. From the distant seaward horizon, muffled claps of thunder peal out, scarcely noticed by the crowds. Wisps of mist find their way onto the pistes and are blown gently by the occasional faint breeze.

The man on the hydraulic lift is wearing a gardener's green overalls and is well sheltered by the trees which he would be trimming if it were his true place of work. He leans the rifle against the backplate of the lift and lines up his sights on the cheering figure on the upper floor of the two-story VIP building. To ensure his success, he lines up the man's heart as he would normally do if he were out hunting rabbits.

The senator is clearly visible in the armchair at the centre of the dais. Beside him, further armchairs accommodate other distinguished visitors, all of whom have been checked out by the Secret Service detail that accompanies him. This is a one-off, as it is rumoured that he will be running for the presidency. Senator Smith's youngest son Alf is playing with a two-handicap. His teammates are also

Americans and have low handicaps, except for the player in position three. His name is Cordoba, a professional player from Argentina with a handicap of seven. It's a no-holds-barred match with mixed amateurs and pros, and Cordoba is paid by the team for participating. His position as player three is that of tactical decider and defence. Alf Smith is number one, primarily offence, and his two fellow Americans, Bud Framer, a lawyer, and Jim Reefs, a stockbroker, both multi-millionaire sportsmen, are position two, a scorer or passer of balls to one, and position four, main defence, who can go anywhere to prevent goals getting through. Just to confuse the issue, every time a goal is scored, the teams change the direction of play.

The game is into its fifth chukker. There are six chukkers in a game with three-minute intervals and a fifteen-minute break at halftime. It's a highly contested match against an all-Argentine team with a nine and a six handicap in their ranks. The competition is intense, not so much for the prize money and trophy as for the winning itself. Sportsmanship is highly valued in this exclusively elitist sector of the equestrian world.

Senator Smith is a highly controversial figure in the political arena. International critics have condemned his opposition to his country's green policies, his intense and lucrative lobbying on behalf of the energy industry, and his contradictory sitting on, and even heading, climate- related committees. The senator's popularity is hardly enhanced by his defence of settler colonialism in Palestine and his known involvement in various highly profitable West Bank projects. Although many say that public opinion has started to go against him, he is strongly favoured by the media for the presidency.

It's a tremendous match. The crowd are up from their seats cheering Alf Smith, who is hanging from his stirrups, his horse going great guns. Slashing through the air, his mallet thuds against the ball which sails straight, and in. It's a goal.

The shooter takes advantage of the pandemonium to squeeze off two shots, and without stopping to check his handiwork, takes the lift to the ground.

Fuck! Fuck! Fuck! The senator is down. Suddenly the dais is thick with running men. It looks like they have grabbed the senator and are running with him. The phalanx of black cars has begun to move, the chaos increased by the settling sea mist. Crowds of screaming people invade the pitches, crossing them in their attempt to escape. The helicopters fly at low levels, cameras whirring in an effort to record all they can. The senator is loaded unceremoniously into a limo, which races towards the exit and the nearest hospital. Armed men lean out of windows and half-open doors of the official cars. The Guardia Civil and Spanish police cars' sirens scream as they follow the motorcade onto the roads around the polo club.

The shooter rapidly packs the weapon and spent casings, stows them on the bike, and returns unhurriedly along the route he arrived by to the N340 highway. He rejoins the heavy traffic, ignoring the screeching sirens and hurtling police and Guardia vans on their way to Sotogrande.

During the subsequent investigation, the inevitable question was asked: "How was an armed man able to get so close, and have the use of a tree lift that was just sitting there?" As usual in a situation where various police bodies from more than a single country are involved, the answers were vague and confusing. The local police responsible for scouring the resort one hour before the senator was due had quadriculated the whole Sotogrande area, but the specific square on which the tree lift was located was overlooked due to a change in shift of the local policemen and women involved. The Secret Service, who also scoured the area constantly, could not explain it, and neither could the agents from various bodies responsible for access to Sotogrande.

ANSAKI DEVOUT

Chapter Four:
The Concentration

The Costa annually suffers a short agony of depression in the winter months early in the year, but once summer arrives, unstoppable activity is heralded in with loud fanfare. A creeping thunder that only slowly awakens your perception, the throaty voices of thousands of motorbikes, the first get-together of everything on two, even three wheels. There is at least one of everything and thousands of some. Scooters, Vespas, Lambrettas, Harleys, the intermittent bouts of revving punctuating the ear-splitting sound of the mass concentration of bikes of every colour and description, even a Matchless, and a Triumph, and Hondas and Nortons and a Guzzi and BMWs, a vintage Indian and a Vincent HRD. They come in their thousands, roaring along the N340 on their way back to Marbella and the Palacio de Ferias y Congresos.

Just as the cavalcade roared along the N340 two-lane highway past the turnoff for Sotogrande, the cacophony created by the incessant revving and the hooting of thousands of klaxons was rivalled by the piercing shriek of dozens of police and Guardia Civil vehicles coming the other way , all hysterically turning off at Sotogrande with a whole fleet of choppers flying in their wake like a bunch of irate mosquitos.

Heading up the massive bike happening were a good dozen Guardia civil bikes, Yamaha FJR 1300s. The guardsmen must have come to the rally to show off their new machines, as traditionally they had lived on BMWs. As the concentration swept past Sotogrande, the mounted Guardsmen, having evidently received news and instructions on their radios, pulled ahead individually, turning off at the next junction and into the oncoming lanes to join the police vehicular presence. Shit seemed to have been let loose in Sotogrande.

Every country seemed to be represented by its own breed of bikers, from groups whose appearance complied with the public notion of what a Hells Angels chapter looked like to Scandies, Germans, Italians, and Spanish, of course. Many flew small national flags in the slipstream of their steeds as they rode. A small group of really smart choppers sporting double sets of unusually long radio antennae at the end of which the flag of free Palestine and the Riffian flag fluttered gaily in their slipstream, joined the cavalcade at the Sotogrande junction and rapidly sped up to replace the Guardia Civil detachment heading the event.

There were five of them, Arab riders, and from what one could make out all were young, well- dressed, and strong. When the cavalcade stopped off in Marbella they motored on through Mijas Costa and on to the urban sprawl of "La Villa Blanca", Fuengirola. They had been down together for the day to the beach by Sotogrande, and each had then gone his own way to scout out different locations an hour before meeting again on the motorway shoulder.

Ali and his brother Salas (short for Salaheddin) wanted to check out the port, Mohamed(nicknamed Hamou) and S'imu stayed on the beach for a while longer, while Afra, the sleepy, discontented loner of the group, opted to check out the polo championship in Sotogrande. They arranged to meet at the motorway junction at seven. Afra was the last to arrive and immediately pulled away.

"Let's go, guys," he hissed. "Let's get out of here. Something very heavy is going down and we will probably be blamed for it, knowing our luck."

In Fuengirola, they left their machines in a lockup they rented, except for Hamou who, being very fussy about his bike, kept it separately, and went to a coffee shop on the seafront where all the young and not-so-young Moroccans, Riffians and Spaniards hung out. The owner, a youngish Rif guy, Aksil, ran it single-handedly, although all of and any one of his clients could become instant waiters at the drop of a hat. All the youngsters were delighted by the way Aksil played the fool and messed around to the gleeful laughs and snorts of his clients, while at the same time keeping an astute hand on the pulse of his thriving little enterprise.

The five drifted in and took seats on the terrace.

"Did they kill him then, Afra? You said they shot him."

"Yeah, of course, they fucking killed him. Must have been two shots." He bent suddenly his face in his hands. "Oh fuck! It was so, shocking. I was there right below where he sat, there was all this shouting and cheering for the game, and yet I heard the thuds. I looked around, you know just an instinct, I saw blood spurt then this guy just crumpled forward. There was like a pause as if time had stopped and then there were guys in black suits, big men screaming everywhere. I ran, and everyone else was running like crazy, screaming. I grabbed my bike and drove like madness across a field and a road and got to the motorway."

"Yeah, they swung out onto our highway and bullied us into one lane. The whole bloody concentration in one lane, and them with dozens of black limos and cops and Guardia cars, and choppers overhead," Ali raved.

"And I saw you there as well, Ali," shouted Afra. "Don't think I didn't see you. I saw you."

Ali studiously ignored him, and while Aksil glanced from Afra to the other, Ali's brother Salas leapt up.

"They were filming us." Salas jumped up to hold a pose for an imaginary helicopter overhead. "Yeah, probably looking for Afra, saw him shoot the guy."

"That's not even funny, Salas," shouted Afra, who was a boy of no more than twenty. He was crying now, and Ali pulled him to his chest.

"He's right," Aksil joined the group, as had most of the youngsters from neighbouring tables. "Look, he's pale, you'd better leave him alone. Relax, it's OK Afra, Salas was just joshing. Don't worry – you were just one of what? Hundreds, thousands of witnesses? No, they're very unlikely to want to interview you."

Hamou and Simu were older and less excitable. They dressed well, had the best bikes, lived well, looked good, and had everyone wondering what it was that they did for a living, although everyone had their suspicions. They, or rather their families, were from the Atlas mountains.

"I'm not surprised they killed him," piped in Hamou. "How long do this lot think they will carry on shitting on the rest of mankind with impunity? My grandfather was an Elder in a village in the High Atlas. Now, they were a democracy, not America who finance terror, shoot minorities, starve their own people." Hamou continued and everyone listened interestedly, as Mohamed always told good stories.

"The Berbers, that's our people, lived in a small community of villages in the high mountains of the Atlas. Four or five of these communities formed a sub-fraction and owned between them an Agadir, a fortified store for grain, and a meeting point for male adults summoned to war. Three, four, or five of these sub-fractions formed a fraction, or canton as the French were later to rename them. The canton was a small republic. A council of the heads of all the families legislated and administrated, and the president was elected annually. The council dealt harshly with crime, imposed fines, and sat in judgment to protect the general interest. Then the French came and screwed it all up, and have never really left anywhere where they once ruled."

"And now it's the Americans?"

"No, Aksil, it's all of them. America and her neighbouring state Canada, the English, French, Germans, Israelis, and others. For me the litmus test is Palestine. What are these people at? If they not only do not raise hell at Israeli genocide, but participate with investment in the stolen territories, sales of arms, and political backing. And the Western media is dumb about everything. They've been got at – even the famously impartial British news corporation is now a Tory conquest. If you don't read alternative press like C... punch then you know nothing of what's going down."

"What about us, the Arab world, and Islam? Surely we are out of their thing?".

"It's not about us, Aksil, it's about our leaders, our big business. We, with exceptions, are as bad as much of the West. Take the United Arab States, a complete sell-out, Egypt, a military dictatorship, and how many have now normalised relations with Israel. No sir, I think people like today's assassin do the world a favour. Perhaps if it became a fashion, to kill off all the corrupt, the child killers, the psychopathic generals in all armies, all patently evil people, each in his community, it would become a counter-current for the good."

"The brothers here don't know what the fuck you're raving on about. They don't understand."

"Of course they don't, they're all too busy chasing invisible girls, acting like tough dealers, and generally fucking about like the rest of this God-forsaken coast. They don't stand a chance. They don't read, and think a book is for standing on a shelf. And they gave up their studies, their only lifeline to a real life."

"How about some tea, Aksil? This a teashop or a school?" chorussed a couple of lads. "Yeah, Aksil," joined in Simu. "How about some of that weak old Harira you dish out?"

"Your money first. Let me see the colour of your dirhams, you lunatics." Aksil jumped up, running off to prepare his orders, screaming out, "Money! money!"

Hamou was a native of The Atlas Mountains, and his father Mohamed was a shepherd.

"Idraren Draren (Mountains of Mountains), this is our home." He would shout it across the empty spaces when he was euphoric, had bought a packet of seeds, and sat smoking them. The animals would eat the bits of grass that grew from the dry, seemingly soilless expanse of mountain. Stupid, senseless shit pellets from sparse grass. Milk and meat and hides for warmth and trade. They stank, but finally, you were one with them. Bleating and panicking madly when the wolf was upon them. They say he strangled or beat it senseless with his fists when he was twelve, later wearing its stinking fur.

When winter came, in the morning the sun would shine upon a coat of thick white snow capping the high mountain. Cold everywhere except where the women cooked; movement, work, or running was the only way to keep your teeth from chattering. The sunlight glittered mysteriously off the massive drifts that had appeared in the darkness of the night. The men would mutter "Alhamdulillah," giving thanks as they did for all those mercies that would enable them to survive in the harsh ranges.

When he was grown his father had taken him down to the great city to learn at the Madrasah. When he returned, he was changed, no longer smoking the weed, and making love to the mountain girl he had married, only to procreate children for Allah. Girls, daughters were sent to him, three girls, Fatima, Malak, and Nurdeeyah. He loved them but they were not the boy he desired. But it was strange that when people years later came and spoke to them of their father, each one spoke of a seemingly different person, a differing personality each with its own likes and dislikes, but they all loved him with a passion.

"Brother, father, friend in Islam, I will leave soon for the frontier between Pakistan and Afghanistan, where the foreign devils of two hemispheres are attacking our brothers and sisters and our world." His friend Amin the Mullah, the Imam of the small mosque in the nearby town, was to be his correspondent and only link to his family. They would sit in the lee of Mohamed's family home where his brothers and his father and all their families lived.

"Wait till the boy comes. Your Hakima is well on the road to giving birth. *Insha Allah* this time it will be a boy. Wait, Mohamed. She will need you."

"Allah needs me more. He has called me many times and I have not gone. My moment has come."

He travelled with brothers, other fighters to be, from many villages of the High Mountain to Peshawar to fight the Russians. But he held his peace and kept his silence, and because of it was respected. His name was Mohamed, named for the Prophet. He went to fight the infidel, the enemy of Islam, whatever his garb and whichever flag he invaded under, his only general Allah and his Prophet.

He knew that God had given him intelligence, the ability to discern good from evil, and his teachers, one in particular, a devout Sufi forever seeking the road to Shahada. His name was Mohamed Al Mahdi. Al Mahdi taught him that in truth religions were all a road to the Light to the beauty and the wonder of Allah. That the devout and sincere, and the seeing in all peoples, all creeds followed the same road. That the true evil infidel was he or she who, on seeing the brilliance of the light shining on the path of Islam, sought to destroy her adepts and faithful.

From Peshawar, they travelled along established routes through sparse villages to cross into Afghanistan, guided and aided by the Pashtuni and sometimes glimpsing those hooded, white- skinned figures they came to recognise as CIA spooks. Mohamed was told by Amin the Iman, his contact in his home village, that his son was born and they had named him after his father, Mohamed. His mother and everyone would call him Hamou, a more familiar form used for the name of the Prophet by people of the mountain.

Running with the goats to the high mountain, warm milk on frozen mornings, and continuous scraps with his cousins and other boys, all of whom ran wild, rosy-cheeked, and strong. Sitting with the sheep to scare off the occasional mountain wolf or wild cat, armed with just a sling and his uncle's staff.

The small Madrasah in the nearby town to learn of Islam and the journey of the Prophet, the Hegira, the teachings, and the Haditha. Amin the Iman and late nights of shared devotion, reading of the Sacred Book, learning of the history of his people, his country, and family. One day, the moment he craved arrived. The Iman dragged him, needlessly as the boy ran but could not keep up, to the tearoom. The men were all standing outside, waiting for them, and nodded sombrely to the priest. The boy had waited all these four years. He had no father as the other boys did, but he was, he knew, the son of a great man, a hero. He knew his father was far away fighting for Allah, and the village and the town knew it, and all the boys, and wherever he went they gave him the respect due to his father.

The military had had a phone installed by the *Office National des Postes et Télécommunications* in the tearoom for their use in emergencies, and over time it had devolved into the town's only contact with the outside world. The room had been cleared when news of the impending call came through, cleared as if Mohamed himself were to appear. They guided the boy to place the receiver at his ear.

"It's your father. Listen and speak to him."

They were hard and simple men from the mountains, the warriors amongst them only ever having left to accompany a Harka(Sultan's army). Now this man, this brother, had gone to fight shoulder to shoulder with the armies of Allah, to fight the hated infidel, and his name had grown in stature, spreading from mountain to mountain. Officials from the city had occasionally come looking for him or his family.

Hamou was alone. His father's absence and the way he was revered placed a wall around him. His only friends were the Iman and his stern grandfather. He craved knowledge even from such an early age. They told him that news of his father appeared in many papers, that he was killing all those who were guilty of hurting the people and especially the children. One day the news came that he had been captured and imprisoned in Pakistan in the fortress of Badaber, close to Peshawar. He was imprisoned with Russians and Afghans fighting the mujahideen of the Jamiat-e Islami party, backed by Pakistan and the CAA. There was an uprising, a siege that resulted in the death of all the inmates. Although it was said that Mohamed had been taken out to be interrogated before the uprising, nothing was heard from him again, and he was given up as having been lost in Badaber.

Hamou, who had only ever spoken to his father briefly on the occasional phone call, grieved for him bitterly. His grief was for the man they had told him he had been: his sisters with their tears and their lost love, their descriptions of what seemed to him to be three different men, his mother, and grandfather and their stories, and Amin the Iman with his gentle praise of a man he said had been pure as the driven snow and brave like a mountain lion. As time passed his father became a mystical part of his being, a wraith, a valiant victim of the evil CIA and their Pakistani allies and traitors to the cause.

The glimpses of his past also formed him, that of his people, father, and grandfather, a tribal warrior. The times they had been called to follow the great Harka, the journeys of the incumbent Sultan into the Bled Es Siba, the country with no law beyond the Atlas, to receive tribute and hospitality from the tribes, or to reduce dissident Sheikhs. The Harka, the burning, it was called, so great was the entourage of the travelling Sultan and the armies, that the area was impoverished, emptied by the excessive needs of the huge gathering and would be unlikely to pose a future threat.

The ruling dynasty left its mark on history mainly through its second Sultan, the brutal Moulay Ismael, who reigned for fifty-five years. The Sultan struck terror in all who surrounded him, as he would often execute servants with his own sword in passing, as a fly is swatted in the lethargic heat of an afternoon. He eliminated many of the foreign enclaves in his country, ejecting the British from Tangiers in 1684 and the Spanish from Larache, wooing the reluctant and incredulous French by demanding in marriage a daughter of their king. Although the country was troubled by civil war for years after Moulay Ishmael's death, Hamou's teachers had taught him that the state would have evolved as all states had it not been for the constant interference of would-be colonisers, among them the Spanish, the Turks, the British, the Germans, and the ones who had most strongly made their mark, the forever devious French.

The treacherous and brutalising French who would tie tribesmen to each other, many of them as young as twelve, and shoot them in the back, the French who later in the Algerian war committed atrocities so many in number and so cruel that they were unequalled in history. But then the Algerians replied in kind, perhaps excelling the French with their practices of carving out the eyes of an unarmed prisoner with a rusty knife to but name one of many. And Hamid, the Moroccan Sultan whom the French deposed, was famous for feeding abject prisoners to the lions, all for the sin of having been successful and popular with the people. Hamou devoured every book made available to him, hauled up on camelback from the great city, and sent by Iman, friends of Amin, and admirers of his father's memory.

As a small-town Iman, Amin had developed an attitude of defensiveness toward the foreign interloper, perhaps wanting to never be quoted, even in error, as an enemy of the Moroccan state. He would teach the boy about things like the Crusades, the Spanish Inquisition, the atrocities inflicted by Christians, to say nothing of the world wars and concentration camps. But the boy held firm in his belief that all people were essentially born pure, and corrupted by Satan's agents walking in their midst. In his forming

41

solitary mind, he was already understanding that the only way forward in any country would be to remove the children of Satan. He was aware of those Mantras in the sacred Koran for the destruction of the evil person.

LAA H'AWLA WA LAA QUWWATA ILLA BILLAAH

Like his father before him, Hamou was taken to study at the great Madrasah. Here in Marrakech, a city he fell in love with, he broke many hearts. A tall, striking man of the mountains, full of his faith, his passion for his people, and hate for those who had for so many years deprived them of their freedom and their peace. Several years later, in 2013, his last year in Marrakech, steeped in Sufism and mysticism, he left Morocco for Afghanistan. For a year he trained for covert warfare, martial arts, weapons, and assassination, a skill that was to prove useful in his chosen career.

Nothing more is known of this person. Many assassinations have been attributed to him, but nothing specific. The suspected killings have been a strange mix, which is why there is doubt as to whether a single or various killers were involved.

Chapter Five:
The Mansion

The daylight arrived from over the hills, stealthily painting with a yellow brush all that it touched. Occasional gleaming whitewashed houses came out of hiding to squat on the Andalusian hillsides, sporting clumps of ragged palm trees and patches of parched fields. The Diez house was shadowed still, while the light slowly climbed the hedges and tree clumps that surrounded it, with its red pillars and sweeping porches starting to materialise in the half-light, accompanied by a cacophony of barking, as the canine sentinels of the little, rustic yet proud would-be mansion broadcast the arrival of the day at their jealously guarded domain.

Sally Anne Diez ran out of the house and flung herself with an abandon born of daily practice onto a deep, wide chaise longue, which her father had strategically placed to face the sun as it came peeping over the tops of the hedges. He moved it each month as the sun changed position so that it would catch the rise every morning. She pretended not to look as Alarico O'Donovan de Medinacheli came running across the fields opposite the house, dodging the hedges and trees to make a last sweaty spurt in a forlorn attempt to cast himself onto the chaise longue and give Sally Anne a dreadful scare. It never worked, she was onto him ages before, but coyly pretended not to have seen him. Only once had she succumbed, and just because she had fallen asleep. She regarded the young man with one bleary light blue open eye.

"Good afternoon."

He bounced himself around to face her. "It's morning, silly. Siesta's later."

"I'll stay then. Wait for siesta." "Come on, it's Saturday."

He bounced himself upright. "I'll grab a shower."

Alarico was just about fair, tall, and slim in an easy-to-fatten-up way. His feet pointed slightly outward when he stood. His eyes were intense, and his features seemed unhappy until he spontaneously laughed and infected everyone he met.

Sally Anne stretched languorously and lifted herself into a sitting position on the chaise longue. She pulled her make-up mirror out from the bag that hung around her neck and regarded herself approvingly as she grinned and smiled and pulled faces. She painted her lips bright red with unhesitant and confident strokes.

Loud Metallica music drew her from the porch and the huge tree of green bananas, one of which she seized and stowed in her bag. She skipped down the drive to an open gate where Alarico lay on the bonnet of an old Mercedes car with very spaced wheels.

"Where are we going, Alaric?" she enquired as she slipped through the open window of the car, *Dukes of Hazzard* style.

"To the beach. It's early enough to avoid the ravenous crowds. I phoned Colia and told him we'd drop by and get him and Peter. "

"Him and Peter, him and Peter again, are they an item, a pair, together, shagging, or is it platonic?"

"I have it on good authority that Plato enjoyed good hearty relationships with his students, and that the Roman parents of the time would send their red-cheeked boys to be educated by the Greek philosophers in the sure knowledge that they would be thoroughly sodomised from day one."

"So it is platonic,"

"No idea – doesn't matter."

Alarico was a doctor and was twenty-seven. He had studied and done his degree. He finally rebelled when he realised that he needed to specialise, to shine a bit and earn decent money, and as a result was still floating around, feeling that the profession had been too dehumanised. The only possibility he was still considering was to be a family doctor, which in Spain was a specialisation.

Running across fields in the mornings was his love. The blood pumping through his body, gentle lopes over grassy hillocks and frenzied leaps across streamlets while the sun climbed, changing from a tiny red orb to a mighty golden dragon. He could hear cockerels hailing and dogs warning as he raced for the unmistakable apparition on the hill that was the Diez house with its aura of greenery and its promise of young warm flesh, tender, sweet, innocent. He knew his power, the wild Anglo-Spanish spirit of the *campo* that came racing like an unspent stallion covering the valleys in jumps and strides. He had had many of the women living in lonely, whitewashed houses. They lusted after him, desired his youth and his beauty, and possessed him in every way they could, and he took them carelessly and ran on.

People said he was strange, full of passion and power, and yet gentle as a lamb and caring. If any animal was ill-treated or not looked after, or child, he would change, rant and rave and threaten. Yes, it was strange – they couldn't put their finger on it, and never stopped to think that perhaps he was a sort of mirror reflecting the less agreeable parts of themselves. They didn´t understand him at all, unable to label him, and they never realised that he did not really know himself, that he was true to his ideas of discipline and did his best to be and live by the sort of code that his dead mother would have expected, and his dead brother would have laughed at.

Many strong influences and personalities had shaped him. His Irish father with whom he now lived, his aristocratic Spanish uncle who had spirited him away on the untimely death of his saintly mother to be educated by the Jesuits. And alongside the memory of his mother, the spectre of his dead brother was forever in his thoughts. Che Ernesto was his name, and his devil-may-care nature had been mainly responsible for his death when he fell from his galloping horse and broke his neck.

Hanging out was what he did, nothing more. There were so many little girls around. They could have been his prey as they walked, surprised by their own unique intelligence and beauty, impressed by their superiority and that of their family and friends. But they all looked at him longingly as he strode by, and he befriended many. A few enjoyed having love made to them in the hot sultry evenings of early summer, those who wanted him just to have had him and preen themselves accordingly for their friends, but then realised that they had never had power over him, that all the power was his.

When there were no girls around, there were always other youths with whom he could go to *botellones* and drink and chat and just hang around with, people who loved to laugh and party.

He had never had her, Sally Anne. She was about his age and breathlessly desirable. Just right at one fifty-seven metres, and slim with soft white skin that bronzed in summer and a face full of sweetness and tousled wild hair. She played with him though, and he let her, knowing that it was the only way he could keep her safe. When the blood ran hot in her she would seek him out and he would comply, allowing her to denude him and to own him in her own way, drawing the line when his unusual sense of decency for both of them was at risk. To him, she was a rock in the wilderness, much as his mother had been for her wild Irish progeny until the death of Che started to eat away at her, and her own eventual decease.

"Where were you yesterday?" she demanded.

"What do you mean?" he retorted lazily, but she didn't reply. They were driving in his mother's old Merc, down to get the others.

"I was with you," he said quietly, to which she did not answer.

"You know I was with you." He pulled off the road onto a layby and down to a secluded spot on the banks of the dried riverbed. He stopped the car and turned to look into her eyes. He kissed her lips lingeringly and inserted his lascivious tongue into her sweet young warm mouth. She, now aroused, pushed her tongue into him only for him to pin it there, to possess her mouth, sucking her tongue firmly. He let her go and adjusted his seat to fall back. They both lay there until she lost the waiting game, returned to seek out his mouth, and then the rest of him until he, at last, ended her passion at the moment that he decided was the limit of decency, or for whatever reason drove him.

It maddened her, but she was chained to him, chained by her unfulfilled desire, her desperate lust for him, her need to feel his love, as strong as the years of negation had made hers for him. And all of this in the uncertain knowledge that he was unfaithful to her, that he had possessed many women in the valley, and still had his way with whoever took his fancy. But it was gossip and hearsay and there was no proof, and anyway, she did not want to believe. She preferred to be sure of his love for her in a romantic way, as a faith, and to explain everything tenuous and nebulous away by tagging him with a label of eccentricity which in her mind could only enhance the way in which she saw him.

She knew other girls and boys did it, some of them daily even, and yet she was hesitant; He had everything to do with it, but her own upbringing and evolving intelligence had led her to dwell on people in history whose lives had been intertwined or even dedicated to ideas of what, to her, were of a dramatically higher order. One of her phases had been reading about and trying to emulate St Teresa of Jesus, of Avila, the mystical philosopher saint. Another, soaking her mind in the spirit of Sufism, alternating a month of an imitation of St Teresa with another on a personal and holy Jihad (struggle) against herself in a bid to achieve instant Shahada, which in fact was meant to take a lifetime of worship to attain. She knew she was different, unique among the girls at school. Nobody there seemed to think beyond the obvious, the mundane and the everyday school curriculum, the technologically governed life, and grins and smiles regarding romance with boys or even other girls. Sally Anne was a loner, an avid reader, and as a result an uninhibited free thinker.

The Merc pulled up at the bus stop by the Mercadona supermarket. Colia, a medium height, smiling, very good-looking Slavic boy waved his hand as Peter, a taller, athletically built Anglo- Saxon guy, opened the car door and they piled in, Peter's hand ever so surreptitiously on the smaller boy's rump for a fleeting second.

It drove Sally Anne crazy wondering who was and who wasn't doing what with whom, simply because perhaps Alarico on some occasion had made active love to either one or both of these

– or even worse, passive love, with his bottom? No, no, she reassured herself, these guys and all of Alarico's friends were all normal guys. But then again, she would muse hours later when the worm returned, what about bisexuality? Perhaps even normal boys could be bisexual?

"Hear about the shooting?" asked Peter.

"God! Don't start on about that again. You must have told half the Costa already."

"Shut up, Colia," hissed the older boy. "I can talk about whatever. Or would you rather I tell them about something else?"

"Don't you dare," retorted Colia, his eyes blazing, "or I'll jump out."

"Come on, guys, you act like a married couple. Stop bitching. Tell us about this shooting, Peter," said Alarico.

"Are you gay?" asked Sally Anne suddenly. "Both of you?" "Why? Do we seem gay?" asked Colia.

"Of course, we're not gay," piped in Peter. "Just interesting. Are you gay, Sally Anne?"

"Well, I've never really tried it, so I suppose I don't know. Many girls say that once you try it it's all you want, so perhaps I´ll not try. I tell you though, sometimes I think that all boys are gay or bi."

"So what about this shooting then, or shall I just stop the car and give everyone a wet French kiss?"

"You can stay away from my ass," said Colia loudly, pouting. "Is a French kiss on the ass?"

"Depends on where in France," answered the Slavic boy, putting on a pointedly feminine accent. "Perhaps that's where I really want to be kissed."

Sally Anne changed the subject.

"So where are we going, to which beach? One of the lonely little spots on the road below Club la Costa. More shingle than sand, but we can run naked."

"Yeah naked is good, you feel good. You can swing in the breeze and brown off your sweet boy's buttocks, and your girl's delicious clams, and mouth-watering melons. Sally Anne, we'll be expecting a total show," said Peter, making a loud slurping sound.

She just sat there swept along by it, laughing with them and enjoying the harmless banter that boys seemed so to delight in, but it always hinged on the homosexual, making her wonder even more. Alarico, she knew, was much more than this. There were depths, and he was highly intelligent and very knowledgeable.

"I wonder," said Peter. "I wonder."

"Don't start," said Colia. "It's about the bloody shooting again? You see Alaric and Sally, this American senator got shot."

"I was just wondering if an Arab did it. All the Arab boys at school seem to be pretty aloof, I mean they walk around speaking their languages and acting like they knew stuff we don't. I always think they're dealers, or secretly violent, but no when you get to know one of them you realise they are just desperate to have a specially outstanding identity."

"That's pretty deep for you, Peter," sniggered Colia, eliciting a punch on the arm from his friend.

"Ahhhhhhhhhhh, he's beating me up again. It's domestic violence. At home today he used his belt." As no one replied or commented, he turned to look pointedly at Sally Ann. "And then he ripped off my pants and tried to insert one of my mother's black puddings into my *trastero*" (storeroom).

"It's *trasero*," (backside) "You moron," said Peter in a monotone.

They stopped the Merc on the highway and took the path down through the rocks to the beach. There were lots of people – it wasn't deserted at all.

"You called it a lonely little spot, and it's full of cattle, Sally Anne, you silly moo." "I was just being poetic. It is August you know. Alaric, what are you doing?"

He had stripped naked, aggressively casting his clothing in all directions, and ran down to the sea shouting. He stopped on the shore and started talking to people, old ladies who walked away.

"Oh goody," screamed Colia, "he's doing his lewd act," as the young Spanish doctor began his repertoire of shocking gigs, including simulations of masturbating exaggeratedly with two hands, screaming in passion as he pretended he was being penetrated, and picking his nose with his toe, while Colia clapped and most people on the beach avoided looking, apart from a couple of wolf-whistlers and some girls who laughed and made suggestions. Someone must have called the beach guards in their white uniforms. Alarico made runs at them, laughing with a false hysterical scream, and then fled into the water when the local police made their appearance at the top of the stairs.

Sally Anne silently gathered up Alarico's clothes and stuffed them into her beach bag. She motioned to the boys and they made for the stairs as the police arrived on the beach.

"Is that your friend in the water?" they demanded.

"No," said Peter and Sally Anne. "*Nyet, nyet*, said Colia. "I am Rasshian, from Rasshia." "Shut up, Colia," snorted Sally Anne.

So they left him swimming out to sea. The police called a patrol boat and by the sound of it a helicopter. Sally Anne and the boys went up the beach steps laughing, in the sure knowledge that he would circle round and emerge at another beach, steal somebody's clothes, and join them, full of himself and laughing like a hyena, at a nearby café.

It was a performance he repeated every summer at one beach or another.

Later, he suddenly got serious and said, "I think I'm going away, somewhere where I will have a meaning, as a sort of missionary. Something my mother and Che Ernesto would have been proud of. Anyway, I think I will have to go."

Sally Anne, who was accustomed to his mood swings, just said, "You mean a lot to us, to me. Why don't we all go off, the four of us?"

"To Morocco," said Peter.

"Can I come with you?" asked Colia, and Sally Anne clapped her hands.

Chapter Six:
The Morgue

I had never met or even seen one in real life, a dead senator that is. He looked, as all deceased people do, small, even shrivelled in death. I could only surmise that the killer had been a professional, or very practiced in the art of shooting, as the blood patch showing where the bullets had struck his garment and entered the body was small and centred just off where the heart was. The clothes he had been wearing had been cast to one side in the first emergency rush.

So, it was a first for me. I had never seen a dead American person, let alone someone as highly ranked within their system as this. Everyone dies, it's the great equaliser. Ironic to think that he spent most of his life doing his best to destroy the concept of equality among human beings

– at least this is what I learned from the alternative press – and that finally a human being had reduced him to the equality of the dead.

There were checkpoints all over the approach to the hospital, but my flashing blue light, and the fact that my beaten-up old BMW was well known to many of them, earned me easy passage and salutes. A shame that security had not been as tight when the killing took place in the afternoon. I had been alerted immediately and made my way without delay straight to the hospital.

The senator had been tubed up, and the attending team of doctors had been making every effort to keep life in the failing body, but prior to even stabilising him in order to operate and remove the bullets, the patient had passed on. He had slipped into a coma, and then they lost him just a few minutes ago.

"I'm so sorry, but he was practically dead on arrival," the doctor heading the team reported as I leaned over the body. "In spite of the fact that the ambulance that brought him in had adequate plasma, the bullets created such mayhem to the heart and surrounds that he bled out, plasma or not."

There were various big, dark-suited Americans in the room, a sergeant of the Guardia Civil, and three guardsmen. The forensic experts and the judge-coroner who would be presiding over the legal case had arrived and taken charge, of certifying the existence of the body and the exact time of death. The forensic and scientific unit of the Policía Judicial then took charge of the official identification of the deceased and the location of any evidence that may have been essential to the solving of the crime, along with detailed and comprehensive photographic evidence of the body, wounds, and lesions to complete the autopsy.

There was nothing for me here.

The Civiles suddenly squared up, and the sergeant smartly yet unobtrusively saluted as a tall, thinnish bespectacled man quietly entered the room. Humble of demeanour and seemingly frail, he was everything he did not appear to be;

this was in no way an act, or the adoption of a seemingly harmless personality to make people relax. I had known him for years and knew that what made him that way was an unusual intelligence combined with a genuinely affectionate personality, although he was a bit of a zealot and could turn officious and even nasty if he felt it was his duty to do so. He turned to the Americans and spoke in halting English.

"I am Captain Jose Garcia with the Guardia Civil, gentlemen. My most sincere condolences."

I left them there as there was little I could add at this juncture. My name is Betardo, and I am from Malaga, Malaga City. My job is chief inspector, *inspector jefe*, of the Judicial Brigade of the national police based in Malaga, and responsible to my *comisario*, who in turn is below the *Secretaria general* in Madrid.

When I arrived at Sotogrande it was like a military encampment.

In Spain, the crime of murder is investigated through the various security and police forces, which are regulated by judges, courts of justice, and the ministry, all in accordance with and following the guidelines specified in the *Ley de Enjuiciamiento Criminal (Law of criminal justice)*.

Immediately after the shooting of the American senator in Sotogrande, the local Guardia Civil, who were already on the crime scene, called for immediate reinforcements, and an area coordinator was appointed. He then set up his task force operating from the *Cuartel* barracks at nearby

Guadiaro. A hotline was set up for cooperation with the local police and, working in unison, detachments of the Guardia and the Policia local cordoned off the whole area of Sotogrande. Within minutes all roads leading out of Sotogrande were closed, resulting in long queues of vehicles trying to leave. Mounted police on motorbikes were pulled off highway duty and from the SEPRONA (the nature protection arm of the Guardia), and controls were set up so that the total perimeter was controlled within minutes of the incident.

I took a look around accompanied by an officer, who pointed out the seat where the victim was shot, on the raised dais on the second floor of the VIP building. Then we crossed the playing fields to the clump of trees hiding the hydraulic lift.

"He got in and out just like that, as if by magic," said the officer.

"No," I replied in a low tone as if speaking to myself. "No magic, just luck and sheer ineptitude on our part and that of the Americans. Not a professional killer, no planning, just intention and opportunity. Probably intelligent and quick-minded. A good polo player, perhaps. Who knows?"

"Did he know the place, sir, do you think?"

"Probably visited some time before. Heard the news about the senator's impending visit and came round for a stroll. It's hardly a private place. Anyone walking their dog would have noticed him, although that's hardly an idea to start looking, as he probably had his own dog along as cover. So, it was just the germ of an idea that started to take root when he came, and then on the actual day of the murder he arrived and went straight to that clump of trees where he found the lift machine. Couldn't believe his luck. He had probably come here intending to climb it."

"We found the key, sir. The operator must have just left it in the ignition. Quite a typical sort of behaviour around here."

"A bad card player often doesn't see a break even if it's staring him in the face. This guy just flowed with it. He won't be easy to track down, probably a total cleanskin with ideals, although ideals do stand out in these social media days, and end up being recorded on some database in Washington. Chances are he's too bright to use social media."

The national police force's judicial body, which can incorporate Guardia Civiles and specialised civilians, then took over. Their forensic experts had already reached the hospital where, with the duty judge, they had certified the existence of the body and the time of death.

So I was in charge from a judicial viewpoint, and would work within the judicial team with Captain Garcia as my Guardia Civil partner; together we would run the whole investigation as we had done so many times in the past. I had a feeling, though, that this case was too politically important to be handled in the normal way, and I wasn't wrong.

As I left the hospital building, a tremendous racket heralded the arrival of two Chinook helicopters that settled on the hospital lawns, flagged in by Guardia Civiles. The American Navy had arrived, most probably to take possession of the body and, who knows, perhaps even the investigation.

Chapter Seven:
The Missive

Wasap – Delaisandra to Rocio: "Hi Rocio, I just got a dodgy-looking email come in. I opened it and thought, what the hell, my anti-virus system costs me enough. Well, it warned me not to open the attachment. I was stupid I know, but it just looked so enticing, forbidden. Then it said stuff in big black letters, UNVERIFIED FORWARDING, this sender is not on your SPF RECORD. And all the rest of the standard warnings and I thought about phishing and spoofing, and what the hell, the worst would be if it blew my computer up, and so, as I'm superstitious or something, I set the cursor over the attachment, got under the table with my mouse and clicked. BOOM!!!... You'll never believe what's in the attachment."

Rocio: "Tell me! Tell me! What is it?"

Delaisandra: "No, you need to come here to see it."

Rocio: "No, I can't. What is it? Send me it for heaven's sake."

Delisandra: "It's amazing, but you need to come here. I'm not answering you anymore, just come, drop everything, tell no one, and come. You've heard of scoops."

My mother and her father shared a big house behind an urbanisation called Riviera del Sol in the Mijas area. It was miles up at the very back, behind the motorway, where various housing developments were abandoned, victims of some recession or other, while the banks that had financed their construction went through the process of repossessing them through the courts, a job that could take years. As a result, it was quite unpopulated and a magnet for thieves intent on scavenging whatever they could get away with at the solitary sites.

We rented the villa from a developer who would one day lose it to the bank, but my grandfather had agreed to buy it when it got to auction, or before if the bank agreed to a big reduction in what was outstanding. Anyway, they had their house, and within the grounds, but separated by a lawn and a garage, was a separate one-bedroom but roomy flat. I also had a nice sunny lounge and a massive terrace, Oh, and incredible sea views. Also, I had my access gate from the street and a garage with a direct and covered passage to my flat. It was far enough from the main house to give me all the privacy I desired.

Given the nature of the location, it was useful to have security, so Grandfather was able to have his dream dogs, Neapolitan mastiffs. They were beautiful and had incredible fur, but if you happened to jump our three-metre high-security wall, that was it, you were dead. If friends came to call, we would close off the part of the gardens where the dogs were, but at night the hounds roamed freely, and woe betide any intruder. Grandfather had posted big signs advertising their presence.

In what seemed like no time, I heard Rocio pull up in her small hybrid Fiat and hoot a couple of times telling me to lock up the guards and collect her. She was panicky about most dogs, so these scared her. I think if you don't show fear and are very slow-moving and relaxed, few animals will attack, and anyway, they knew her.

We sat out on the terrace where the scent of jasmine was most noticeable. Arabic jasmine, not Cuban – all the visitors ask. The Cuban version, *Alamanda catharica*, is on the other side of the house. It's an aggressive creeper with beautiful yellow flowers. Grandfather smuggled in some seedling plants.

Rocio got quite upset when I told her about the contents of the email.

"You're fucking crazy. You should go straight to the police. It's not a game, you know. The guy's a killer, and the whole world is looking for him."

"The whole world? The whole world has no idea of who was responsible for the murder. They're running around like bears with blindfolds. The Policia Nacional, the Guardia Civil, and these guys are good, the best, they had years of experience with ETA. And this is unique, it's a passport to world coverage, international fame if we play it right."

We were two young female journalists. One, I, was very young, at the start of my career. The other, Rocio, had never really had a proper career but just floated along, and although from a prosperous and influential background, she was a declared if somewhat theoretical enemy of radical capitalism.

I hadn't thought everything out. I was just too busy at first with my studies, changes in my life, and my mother and grandfather, but one thing I did know was not to look a gift horse in the mouth, another of Grandfather's many sayings. Rocio may well not have been a battle- hardened war journalist, but she was much more experienced than I was, and I knew that she would become more fervent about the idea as time progressed simply because it would be one in the eye for men. This is the email I showed her that got her going. I had read the whole press release three times over, but didn't let on.

Hello.

I am sending this to you with the expectation that you will use your knowledge and ability to put it before the eyes of the world. I know this is not an easy task, but anticipate that you will confront it with passion, given that at some juncture it will make you one of the most famous journalists in the world. I do not think it will give you problems, at least no more than those created for Julian for speaking too loudly, jajajaja. It is truly very sad and wrong – after all, he only spoke the truth.

Who am I? That, you will hopefully never know. All you need to know is that I am the instrument that was used recently to terminate the life of Senator Smith. The following is a press release crafted by me, which we require that you do not alter in any way. I will be attentive to how my script reaches the press and how extensive is the coverage you can achieve. I suppose that Western media will shy away from publishing the script, but will eventually accede once the alternative press, internationally, gets hold of it, and it goes viral on the various social media networks, as it will if properly handled.

I will not place conditions on who you share our secret with, as if it becomes impractical to use you, or if we do not get the cover required, I will approach an alternative journalist to carry out the task.

ANSAKI DEVOUT

Chapter Eight:
Ansaki. First Press Release

I have killed a man today. I am associated with no group or body, just me, a noble savage. My victim, a person whose corrupt manipulations, whose abuse of power has brought the world closer to destruction, and who needed to be stopped, has now been terminated.

I hope that the world learns why this act took place and that it is intended as the start of a balance for the evil this person has created. To this end, I will do my utmost by employing international press releases to advertise this happening. Western media will drown the news or attempt to. Hopefully, such an effort on their behalf will be futile.

The CAA murders people every year. How many exactly we will never know. It may be by using drones, or a bomb strike, or direct assassination, or whatever method is convenient to them. The CAA is therefore a mafia. A criminal organisation? An evil secret society? Yes, but it belongs to and works for the American government, therefore it is a legitimate operation.

It, therefore, follows that all foreign governments who enjoy friendship and solidarity with the said American State can also, and do, murder and commit crimes at will, as is the very remarkable case of the so-called Middle Eastern democracy, a state that has murdered, apart from thousands of adults, children, in many cases little children, and continues to do so in the present.

If we go back in time in lots of 10 years, we will see that accountability of the state to population and law has diminished radically in increasing leaps every so many years, so that today most governments do not even pretend to operate according to the rule of law.

Well I, as a normal, decent enough person with certain standards that I live to, am sickened by what I see going on around me. Also, people seem blind to what is happening. When I have challenged different individuals with for example Yemen, they give me answers like,

"Bloody Arabs, they start it and then..." or "Nothing to do with me mate..." or

"Look, I have enough problems of my own..."

Then of course there are the "inane" who seem to be multiplying in numbers as the years pass us by. They are the ones who populate the so-called "social media" and fly to excuse irresponsible billionaires or corrupt politicians every time an intelligent criticism is levelled at any of them.

In 1958, that's just 63 years ago, Yemen was a backward country, ruled over by an Iman from the Zaidi Shiite tribes. At the time, the British Empire and the USA were busy squabbling over how the Middle East should be divided up. What struck me most of all was the general ineptitude of all the British and American players, with few exceptions. The result, 63 years later, is that the population is still suffering hugely at the hands of the new would-be owners of Yemen, Saudi Arabia, the Arab states, and their partners in crime, the American state. In their usual ponderous and inept fashion, the Americans are illegally blockading the country, so that Yemeni children in their thousands are starving to death. What a way to win an argument – blockade and kill off the population. Clumsy and evil, yes patently evil, and the Woden Administration knows full well the terrible effect of its politics.

And we have the ME democracy? which is perpetrating an act of genocide against the Palestinian people. Perhaps it's all a sham, and all the thousands of evidentiary videos that appear day by day are a lie. One hell of an elaborate and unlikely lie. And I in my ignorance ask myself, why can't they just find a simpler way?

And the demise of the planet, made imminent by some politicians with interests in industries that are killing the globe, yet do they pull back and change things? No, they kill off the opposition to their companies, they interfere in the affairs of countries all over the world, for greed. This greed is a form of madness, and so now, is my dedication to providing a balance of sorts for this madness. It is only me at present, but perhaps there are others and we are not told. The world press keeps mum.

Ansaki. Press Release Part Two 30.3.2022

A new war has begun to add to all the other wars being waged on the planet for no purpose other than to feed the egos and power of the small-minded men and women behind them. The wars together with the many excesses practised all over the planet by corporations, oligarchs, plutocrats, billionaires, and generally evil and depraved persons must stop and must stop NOW. Top scientists give us 20 years to reduce our emissions to 50% of the present, and we the Ansaki intend that this will be achieved and that all of those who are found to, without a shadow of a doubt, be sinning, continuously and radically against humanity will be sanitised.

To be Ansaki, a person must have studied for at least five years and have some sort of qualification that sets them apart. A sanitisation must be only of an individual who has been studied for years and who meets the criteria of being a criminal, corrupt, and whose actions bring evil and pain and suffering to the human race and especially its children.

Sanitisation is not an act of evil if it is carried out for all of these reasons. Our rulers in many countries have lost their authority to rule us by allowing people to die of disease, causing wealth to be stolen off the state in such volumes that the people go hungry and live in poverty, having no access to clean water, clean air, or otherwise. When a ruler or ruling body lose their authority for reasons of immorality, then they empower the Ansaki, heart in hand and seeking the approval and benediction of their God whoever he may be, to carry out the long-term examination and investigation, and if the subject proves guilty of such evil, to sanitise him or her for the wellbeing of the planet, and so that transgressors who do not toe the line out of fear of their God, will do so out of the fear of just retribution by the Ansaki in the name of their own God.

For he is the minister of God to thee for good. But if thou do that which is evil, be afraid; for he beareth not the sword in vain: for he is the minister of God, a revenger to *execute* wrath upon him that doeth evil.

Now here in Romans 13.4, St Paul speaks of the right of rulers to punish evil. The world though has turned on its axis and it is the rulers and the powerful who are doing the evil. The individual is therefore obliged to act for the preservation of everything.

Perhaps I will be pronounced mad by some, and who knows it may be so. I know there are moments in the dead of night when despair grips me, as in killing this man and the others I will later deal with, I am acting on what I believe I must, and in accordance with my duty before God.

People may say that whether this man was good or evil is a matter for each individual to work out for themselves and that for some, he may be a hardworking businessman and politician, and for others, he may be a corrupt and scheming devil. A matter of personal conjecture they may term it, but I have studied this person's movements and acts for years now, and feel that for mankind to survive, he and persons who act similarly cannot be allowed to continue, and hopefully my action and the actions of the many who will join me in my crusade will be successful in dissuading future politicians and people of power against such sort of behaviour.

That it is presumptuous to assassinate a person in this way, that only the law or God above have the right to take a life, yes, but these people have placed themselves above the law, which they manipulate to their constant advantage and to guarantee their impunity, to the extent that rule of law has been more or less lost. God helps those who help themselves, and evil has prevailed so many times and so blatantly throughout history, that if now, today in 2022, unnamed persons, acting in the name of humanity take it upon themselves to remove the cancerous individuals in our midst, I am sure we will do so with God's blessing.

'Insanity is rare in individuals: but in groups, parties, nations, and eras, it tends to be the rule.' (Friedrich Nietzsche)

If our acts of sanitisation become common and frequent, they may bring chaos; but what greater chaos than today's plastic-choked world, where every year that passes brings us closer to the death of our planet or Armageddon?

That evil persons of stature and wealth may hide away in walled mansions, private islands, or even in space, in another world that we cannot penetrate. But no man or woman is an island, none of us can live alone, and it will be seen that the Ansaki will rise everywhere; they could well rise up in the very bosom of your family, closest friends, or retainers; remember Brutus.

There are indeed hundreds of thousands of potential anti-state idealists out there, the majority of whom have a price on their heads and are wanted by secret government agencies all over the world. The Ansaki are pro-government and pro-freedom and stability. The sanitisation any Ansaki may carry out may make him or her subject to intense investigations and manhunts, but the design and reasoning behind any such action by the Ansaki are to protect mankind.

So why will the Ansaki not fall under the world government's scrutiny? The Ansaki are total loners, completely unaware of the existence or identity of other Ansaki – the greatest fear of all security bodies, a lone wolf, a total cleanskin.

But let me tell you one thing, which only some among you may grasp at first, and others only later as the game begins to evolve. Given that the Ansaki will be highly intelligent, well educated, and passionately idealistic individuals, as they carry out their Deity-inspired tasks, it will be instinctive for them to plot and anticipate the positive effects that their acts will bring to humanity, locally, nationally, and globally. At the same time, other emerging Ansaki will also look to the last published amputation, and previous ones, to inspire their own assassination effort and to plot it so that an end will be created as a result of acts happening everywhere. Like a giant plotted chess game all over the globe, it will become a huge social movement dedicated by its very nature to the elimination of evils that may harm and threaten mankind.

Of course, the Ansaki will produce their own villains, wayward Ansaki, who will, in turn, need to be detected and stamped out by other Ansaki. That the very nature of the Ansaki itself may go evil? Yes, but I argue that to do so, the rogues will move away from the purity of individuality and form groups which will be their undoing as they will become sitting ducks for new pure, emerging Ansaki.

There have been assassins throughout the history of mankind but in the majority of cases inspired by power and wealth-mongering. There have been those killings inspired by altruistic and noble motives, but never has a pattern evolved because it has never dawned on humanity that such a thing could be the way forward.

"He's a lunatic, a total raving nutcase," Rocio said very quietly after they had sat there in total silence for at least half an hour, just watching the sun go down over Africa. "But he's also highly intelligent. The bit about the chess game, it's feasible and..."

"But Rocio, do you actually see people lining themselves up in droves to be Ansaki? People today are too..." the other woman cut in.

"Too what? We'd get armies of them. The trouble is that he wants intelligent idealists, free thinkers, and good people. Yes, they are there, and they would come forward. Well, not come forward, but entertain the idea, select an evil person near to home, and become a sort of sleeper, a spy. The idea is of course that they never get caught, but they will, in many cases. What will be interesting for candidates is whether *he*, the Sotogrande killer, gets caught or not."

"He'll get caught, they always do. Remember he's a loner. That's the hard part, but I agree with what he says, it's the loneliness that will keep you pure. Imagine, you just massacred a top politician, a person, a warm-blooded human being. Nobody to talk to about it and it's killing you. You rant, you rave, you cry, and it's the first person you've killed ever. You vomit, you're sick, over days, weeks it gets to you, also you're shit scared, the world is looking for you.

So you turn to your God, nowhere else to turn. Slowly you begin to reflect more on the spirit of why you carried it out. You scan the press and internet, you look at the deceased's political party, running mates, policies, and companies, and you see or imagine you see the ripple caused by his death. He will want to further the positive direction of that ripple, another sanitisation, and that will be his undoing, he'll get caught."

"No he won't, Dalai. I'll tell you what he'll do, he'll publish his findings, provide a road for a new Ansaki to follow, and start the chess game off."

"Well, we'll see, and don't call me that, makes me sound Buddhist." "What, Dalai? It's your name. He could be a psycho?"

"No way. Read the press release again. This guy cares, it's what drives him. No way a psycho."

They sat there in silence both of them looking out to sea. A dense mist clouded the far-off horizon, hiding both Africa and Gibraltar. The distant sound of muffled claps of thunder that emerged from the mist cast an air of mystery on an otherwise sunny day. They were both deep in thought trying to grasp the reality of the situation.

"We should hand it to the police?"

"To what end? The cops are useless. We're more likely to discover the guy's identity than they ever will. Look, Dalai, I'm the one with the influential family and I am Spanish, but I think we should keep this to ourselves, and for more reasons than one."

"You mean he has a point, you mean we need something like this. That evil has taken hold even in our little world of press and media, that Western media is silent, corrupt, and partisan. The West never learns of the atrocities or the true situations in most of the world, it just is not reported. Palestine, the bombing of Gaza, daily murders, assaults on holy shrines, illegal imprisonment, even of little children with no charges, the list goes on and on; and now it's about local evil, starvation of people in countries of the West, and the country is not told. The results of noninformation or even fake news all the time create multiple evils. Among them, I think it was Orwell who said that it would result in the loss of critical thinking and resultant self-expression in people."

"And so what, are we to hope our Ansaki goes and hits a press baron? Sets his killing as an example?"

"No, of course not. We just need to be a bit like *Return to the Future*."

"Hahahahaha, that's certainly a way to look at it. We cannot change the future, or we should not. Are you saying that this person is a natural evolution of what is going on, and we as information professionals should just do our job and keep out of what actually happens? That's rich. OK, let's get cracking then. We need to get this press release out by every means possible – and even the impossible ones. And anonymously, of course.

They were good at their job. Two days later the press release started to appear. Few major Western papers ran it, but it appeared in the alternative press and started to go viral on every technological media service, and as it gained momentum the major news services were obliged, to avoid loss of face, to carry articles, interviews, opinions by politicians, psychiatrists and psychologists. Police chiefs appeared as interviewees on major TV shows throughout the world, and the assassinations began.

ANSAKI DEVOUT

Chapter Nine:
Los Viejos

August had been hot, hotter than ever, for as long as they could remember. The viejos(Old men) sat on a tarpaulin spread on the sand in the shade, in the lee of their fishing pateras, which were hauled up high on the beach. They smoked ducados and talked about the unusual weather. It was also memorable because it was in August, just a few days or weeks ago, that someone killed the Senator, the American Senator. The smell of old fish mixed with salt and tobacco hung over the boats. The old men had fished here for generations, and their fathers before them. They had seen the bloody civil war and known the hunger, la Hambruna, that had come with it. It had been so bad that during adverse weather spells when fishing was impossible, the men of the boats would go into the countryside to forage for figs or whatever could be found. They were driven off by surly shouts, the occasional rock thrown as a missile, and screams of "Return to the sea, Marengos." So, the families of the sea were tight clans forced together by need, and by the might of the sea – los Marengos.

And then the regime and Franco slowly emancipated them, and they made houses for the families along the beach, "las Protegidas." A change came, and they went to school to be beaten by priests. Tourism came, and great prosperity for the rich, and the banks followed to see how they could take over. And the old fishermen sat in the bars and drank their Anis del Mono and went to work as well they could in an overfished bay, and on many an evening sat by their boats on the sand, repaired their nets, and talked of what had been and what was to come.

"He had so many bodyguards, so much police and Guardia Civil. All the searching and stopping people, it made a mess of the polo. Spoiled it for the season."

"What polo, Jose?"

"The polo! The polo! You know, the championship, with the horses and the sticks and hitting the ball. Oh! Of course, you are from Sevilla – you only know about the fair."

"Did they get him, the killer?

"Did they get him? No of course they didn't. They're useless. Not like in Franco's day. So many officials, police, Spanish and American, troubling the visitors."

His friend chortled. "Don't let your son hear you say these things. Jajajaja. Anyway, they say he had it coming."

The fisherman blessed himself. "Don't talk ill of the dead."

"He never paid any tax, his companies destroyed nature, and he was responsible in the government of America for protecting the air and trees, and the sea, and he used his power to screw nature."

"But you can't just get a gun and go and shoot a man just because he pays no tax and because he destroys trees. It's a sin, it's wrong."

"Well, no, we can't, we don't. We sometimes feel like killing someone, anyone, in the street, a guy who cuts you up, especially now in the heat, but do we do it? No. But suppose he killed your family, like happens in Palestine or Iraq, and you knew it, then would it be, ok? Anyway, let me tell you one thing, these guys steal, but not like before, now they steal not millions, but billions of dollars. Billions, do you know what a billion is? It's one thousand million. And they're all at it, chasing after the billions; the result is that the working people have no medicine, get less pay, and many starve."

"Like in Los Boliches."

"Que dice (what are you saying), Jose?"

"For years the dogs in Los Boliches have had sticking-out teeth, every dog you see, all with these teeth, ugly, because generations before there must have been a really sexual dog with champion genes and sticking-out teeth who mated with every bitch in the town and scared off the competition."

"Y Que? And what?"

"That's what your billionaires want, Epifanio."
"Descendants with sticking-out teeth?"

"Well, they want the poor and weak not to reproduce, to die off so that the future will have only their descendants, like Genghis Khan, like the Bolichero dog. I only say it, my opinion. I don't know, I am just a fisherman. They tell me that the real knowledge is in books, good books of course.

I never read a book. I don't know how to read, a book, that is – yes I can read, but this business of sitting there and reading a book needs to be learnt. But I say, I am not sure if this is the way, this killing of big scoundrels. but I have a feeling we are going to see lots of it, lots of killings."

"Si hombre, don't be so dramatic, Jose,"

"No, of course, but they are going too far, and there are always people, you know people who you never imagine will do something, solitary wolves who will act and perhaps set off the unexpected."

"Like the man who started the First World War by killing a duke. We learned it in school – he was eating a sandwich."

"That's stupid, why would he eat a sandwich? You mean, when he took the shot, or are you talking about the duke?"

"Maybe because he was hungry, a hungry wolf, a solitary hungry wolf. The killer, I mean. Don't try to confuse me. You do it on purpose Jose, it's becoming a habit, you even do it to your son. You're lucky he is so patient."

With the cooling of the day at seven, la hora de la fresquita, they were joined on the tarpaulin by Jose's son, chief inspector, inspector jefe, of the Judicial Brigade of the national police, Juan Betardo Solis. After giving his father the customary two kisses and shaking hands with Epifanio, Juan Betardo, now in plain clothes, sat down with the two older men, on a beach chair not benefitting from the shade of the pateras as did the viejos, but the sun had lost its intensity and did not trouble him. He hailed a boy from the nearby chiringuito or beach bar shack, who brought him a granizado de limón, fresh lemon juice with added sugar, completely absorbed by crushed ice, and some hierba buena (mint). Curro, the owner would always growl, "Not the shit they give you these days. They call it a smoothie, coloured chemicals with minutely crushed ice, tastes like powdered chemicals with lots of sugar. No, Señor, here in my house we serve only home-crushed ice with home-squeezed lemon from my finca."

"I am very tired, Papa. They are exhausting me with their politics and their abuse of the established chain of command."

At the lack of any response from his father, who just sat there, reclining in the lee of the patera, his face partially covered by an old straw hat, and the clumsy efforts of Epifanio to fade into the background as unobtrusively as possible, Juan continued with his monologue.

"Papa, they have brought in a forensics team from Madrid, a woman who they say is the top in the country, with a team of mainly women. Well, my people are having to work with their colleagues from outside, of course. They are all national police. And Jose Garcia and I have now got this very assertive female profiler-investigator to work with. I wouldn't mind, but we need to be very careful in all that we do and say, and at the slightest faux pas she starts throwing her weight around in a very sneaky way. She is good, but it's all cramping our style.

"Oh, and to add to it all, a strange turn of events. The deceased was a strong supporter of the massive funding of the so-called Middle East democracy, so we now have a team of secret service people from the said country here as well, investigating on their own behalf, with the tacit approval of the Spanish government. All we need now is an American warship in the bay as a base for a team of investigators from the deceased's own country.

'Papa, please say something."

The old man came to life. "I would, Juan, I would, but don't know what you are talking about. You sometimes forget that I am just an old fisherman."

"Venga, Papa, come on, say something."

"Juan, you, are the Inspector Jefe, both you and your friend Jose have brilliant minds, so please don't come here to insult Epifanio and I with all the soap opera content. If you want to discuss, then tell us what you are up to, you and Jose, forgetting all the bomberos toreros(fireman bullfighters, a comic circus troupe)."

The chief inspector sat there deep in thought. After a long silence, he looked around. He was an attractive man with a long nose, big brown eyes, high and well-set apart cheekbones, and a forever ready smile that had creased his mouth and lower features into a "Cara de bueno" (good person's face). He glanced in the direction of Epifanio, his father's friend.

"Epifanio is a tomb," grunted the old fisherman. The policeman appeared not to have heard but continued with his discourse.

"Most international police and secret service bodies are very paranoid about individual secret actors like this killer. The popular term is lone wolf or cleanskin, denoting the fact that the person is unknown to them, and is just emerging from the darkness and will return there. Three days ago, two soldiers from the Middle East democracy were both killed, over in Morocco. They belonged to a sniper unit well known for their taste in shooting young Palestinian men, and boys, in the knee, for no crime other than participating in protests. The secret service squad we have here now, from the Middle East country, was in Tangiers to investigate the murder of the two soldiers, and have come here as they believe it's the same killer as in Sotogrande.

"Well," cut in Jose, "it's the Jews. What do they expect? They've been killing these people, their own people historically, their distant cousins, since 1948."

"Not Jews, Papa, Zionists."

"But they're Jews. I know a few Jews and they hate Israel and all that is happening, or so they say, but then they go there on holiday.

"And in other places, it's also happening. Across the English Channel, a news agency chief with a reputation for muting or tainting all news relating to the illegally imprisoned

Australian journalist has gone missing, and foul play is suspected.

"The young fellow with the children and the strong woman, it's a conspiracy against him. Fine young man, wonderful woman – they should be ashamed. This is worse than Franco's times. So now they've done in one of the gang, and right here in Sotogrande. Serves him right as far as I'm concerned."

"But Jose, they can't just go around shooting people," blurted out Epifanio. "Calla ya, Epifanio, be quiet now."

"Papa, even in Spain there have been death threats made to various persons, including an overzealous bank official, a civil servant with a dubious reputation for misinforming old people concerning the true urbanistic value of their properties, and a teacher over-enthusiastic in his advice to young boys as to the value of the anus as an alternative sexual instrument."

"Well, the teacher – if I had a gun I'd shoot him myself."
"Papa, coño, joder."

"No son, no, I respect everybody, they can do what they want, but the children, they leave the children alone, poor little mites."

"The scary part is the speed at which the copycats appear to have acted and to be acting in other areas. Dozens of them. The Sotogrande killer's press release seems to have had a much greater effect than originally anticipated, so we are under pressure to nail the organism or method of distribution of the release as much as the killer himself. The fear of course is that the idea will continue to propagate at its present or an increasing speed.

"We understand that most of the emerging or new Ansaki, that's what the murderer calls himself Papa, are showing intent to spread the word, as it were, or to attract new converts to the idea. So far, adepts with their press releases and who have actually committed murder have appeared in most Western countries. The targets are, in the main, powerful people. To give you an idea, the following individuals have been assassinated: the CEO of a major petrol multinational that was involved in creating natural disasters in more than one South American country. Three British politicians involved in the corrupt handling of the dismantling of the health service in the UK were shot by someone. Also In the UK, the CEO of a water company had an accident. In Russia, one very rich and powerful man, a friend of the president, an oligarch. Oh, and two American billionaires were shot down whilst travelling in the same helicopter. Detectives are at a loss to understand how the killer hit the right craft with their surface-to-air missile when there were two decoys. The worry is of course that the killer may be someone within the inner echelons of their organisation. It is also noteworthy that these two businessmen were the brains and dynamo behind a special anti-Ansaki task force that was being set up by a group of wealthy businesspeople and politicians.

"America is apparently in a state of chaos, the official media tell us, but then we hear otherwise, that things are running very well, better than ever. The likeliest targets for 'justice killers', as they have begun to call the Ansaki in the States, are leaving the country in droves. The same but to a lesser extent in Canada, where up to seven top executives in the mining industry have been shot. In the States, the killings are in every imaginable field, and we have no official tally. What we do know is that at least ten top persons in the armaments world have been assassinated.

"Oh, and in China, we understand that two Ansaki assassinations have been committed, in a small city of five million, and the authorities have promptly sent in the army and closed the city down. But this has not stopped the phenomenon, as two further such incidents have been reported in the country.

"Brazil has seen a spate of Ansaki-type killings, mainly of corrupt politicians, bankers, and businesspeople involved in major projects threatening natural resources and the rainforests.

"And the list continues, banks, politicians, and industrialists in many countries. There is one very comprehensively documented story, and press release that is highly likely to be false and misleading. This is the story, and we have gleaned that it is set in Saudi and Somalia, or so we suspect. I think this story will touch you, Papa. There's so much evil in it, and these, the protagonists, are two men who are dealing in their own ways with that evil."

Chapter Ten:
Ismael

It's so vivid. I know it's just my imagination. I see the mother in the marketplace. She goes by as in a trance from which there is no awakening. She looks like a ghost. I don't know how she is still alive. I don't know how I still am alive, for that matter. I don't think it's just hate, I think it's that I owe it to him, and to what there was. I owe it to remove those responsible in any way and set an example.

I cannot even tell you where I am, but it could be anywhere in that part of the Arab world that is favoured and used by the Western world as a weapon against the rest. These are Arab countries that pride themselves on being progressive and defenders of democracy and modernisation. If I am to preserve my secrecy as an Ansaki I must be careful, as these secret services employ people with the instincts of rats, and now today they have at their disposal the technology sold to them by the Israelis. From the moment my press release becomes in any way visible in the press or on social media, they will set their whole investigative apparatus in motion to find me. I understand that the power of the Ansaki will come from the inability of security forces worldwide to identify us. Some will fall, it is the law of averages, but on the whole, we will be a shadowy collection of vigilantes all over the world, hopefully forever growing in numbers to be as multitudinous as the wheat in the field.

She loved him so much, always in her stern devout woman's way. Ishmael, he was so beautiful. I say was because he must be dead, the newspaper reports must be true, but I have not seen his body. Better he be dead than in the hands of those monsters. He had that way, the manner in which he shook his head with enthusiasm on meeting someone, his laugh, so infectious and always inclusive, the way he would stand up smiling for everyone. His hair was short but long enough for a page boy sort of top so that when he shook his head his hair went charmingly with the motion. And It was that thick or rather dense or strong blondish hair, and his boy smiles and golden eyes that flashed with delight, that made the blood rush to my head whenever I saw him.

I noticed it happening right from the start, but I did nothing. After all, I was a, what is it they call us in the West? A stalker. He was still at school, the youngest of four brothers. I had watched him now for three years since he was 17, and I loved him with all my being, although I had never spoken to him or even been near him. He was quite short but beautifully made, no more than one hundred and seventy centimetres, perfectly proportioned with a delightful, gently protruding behind. His skin and complexion were smooth and white, with an off-tan that made him look more like a European or South American than the fruit of the mixes of Arab blood that he was. But I, who truly loved him, was doomed to never be with him thanks to the brutal laws against gay people in this country.

In my terrible frustrated loneliness, I scoured the internet for years to find a boy like Ismael to be able to consummate my love with and set my devils to rest. That is when I found Jamaal.

Jamaal

(I am also, myself, narrating Jamaal's story based on all that he told me, with enough evasion and distortions for him never to be suspected.)

It was rank, and the smell of ammonia permeated everything. He quickly took the pot and emptied it into the gutter outside the hovel they called home. He watched the urine trickle along the hardened mud of the ground. The old woman looked at him with unseeing eyes. She sat there all the time, every day, waiting to die. She would say to Jamaal.

"Speak to him, to Allah. He will answer you. She is your mother If you ask him he will help you, but you must believe, must know that he will."

So Jamaal knelt some days for an hour or more.

"She's dying, so slowly. My God, can't you help her?" God helps those who help themselves.

His father had tried everything. He was exhausted, working many hours for practically no pay and coming home to care for her.

"It's only a respiratory infection. Only, they say, but it's killing her. No one has much money, all my brothers. For what purpose have brothers if they cannot, will not help?

91

And without money, the doctor will not save her. May Allah bring his rightful wrath to bear on those devils who came here from America to start the troubles, to steal the little we had."

Jamaal opened the windows to clear the air. She moaned, and he went to her and put his palm against her forehead. "God will help, you, you will see." She smiled up at him. "You are so big, Jamaal, so handsome, and only seventeen. You will be a good man." Then she coughed the awful, racking sound that he knew was to be her death knell.

He knew he was not big, about 166 centimetres, and this was why he was often bullied. The other reason was that he was beautiful. He knew this from the girls and the women. He took no notice of them, but some men would lewdly wink at him. He had considered the possibility, of course, many boys had, with a foreigner, but it was illegal and dangerous, and all of these local men who looked at him were dirty and unkempt and lived in hovels. The whole idea was repulsive to him, especially as he attended the mosque. The brothers there also wanted to help his mother, but since the war had started, years ago, there was nothing – just illness, death, and starvation.

It was his uncle's idea. "There's only one way we can save her."

"You are a dirty Shaitan, Kader." His father had grown very angry. The veins on his head stood out, and Jamaal thought they would burst. A big man, strong and driven, shackled by his undying love for the woman who lay sick in the bed. Not so long ago they had been happy.

"It's all we have, Allah knows."

"Don't you dare to mention Allah. Allah is great and good."

The long bus ride to the coast with his uncle dragged on. Mile after mile of desert was slowly hauled past.

He thought of what the man would do to him. He was afraid, of the man, of the pain, and he was repulsed and disgusted. But his uncle had told him that he would need to act like a loving and obedient girl towards the man. To use his hands and his mouth and his tongue and to say nice things, and to let the man have his way even if there was pain. But he was a boy, and as a Muslim student in the mosque, he had been taught that such things were evil. But what horrified him was that sometimes when it passed through his mind graphically, his mind of its own volition kept calling back the thought, like a tongue seeks out a wounded gum or a loose tooth and touches it again and again.

He thought about it so much that he began to think that he felt a pleasurable anticipation. He thought he felt his manhood thicken, and put his hand there as unobtrusively as possible, unsure of the reality.

Did he want it? Was he a *habarr a Zemen*? No, he was saving her life. An image of her flashed into his mind, and he remembered the rank smell, the bucket. "Allah, all of this is wrong, everything, the poverty, the violence, the hunger, people dying. Allah, show me your way, I implore you. "

The bus made its seemingly desultory way through the outermost fringes of the large town. The cluster of closely packed buildings spread in all directions, topped with the occasional minaret and structured conception of the mosques. In the near distance, a coastal road entered the town along the front, and beyond it, spread in all its wonder, the glittering beauty of the cobalt sea speckled with dozens of what slowly changed from myriad insects to boats large and small. And on closer scrutiny, the nearer one drew, some with masts and others with cabins housing their motors, and coloured headscarves, some flying in the breeze, others flapping, trying as it were to escape from the black and brown coloured figures who used them as clothes.

The uncle, Kader, had been the arbiter of Jamal's doom, the purveyor of his beauty via some website or other found by him and his mate, the local computer shop manager. The internet shop was a throwback to 25 years ago when mobile phones were still a relative luxury and not at the world's disposal. The manager had some nasty friends and was reputed to have had something to do with the disappearance of a good number of the more nubile young boys and girls of the town.

The interested party was a good man. An errant Muslim somewhat lost in the mysteries of the flesh and the demons they inspired in normal human beings. It had been the photo, and then the many others that they had hysterically sent on to him as the money suddenly started to materialise in the local Western Union shop, which seemed to have galvanised the punter into action after a slow initial start. The more he saw of the boy's images the faster he promised to come.

"A good Muslim," sniggered the internet shop manager, a good Muslim who only wants the boy's arse." The boy's uncle had many a good laugh together with his friend.

"Ask for one hundred American dollars," the words slid off his tongue luxuriously. To Kader, money was a mythical object, something that disappeared when you touched it.

"Kader, the bus tickets will have to be paid, and you need a cheap hotel there when you arrive, and surely you don't want to give away the goods for free?"

Jamal knew that they had finally settled on five hundred American dollars and that his uncle Kader was to collect half on meeting the man, and the rest after Jamal had spent what was left of the day and the coming night with him.

The bus stopped constantly once it got to the town, letting off passengers who had finished their journey, and being flagged down by new travellers. People were very friendly and talkative, and the banter was nonstop. Jamal was by the window gazing out across the streets while his uncle sat on the aisle seat, his back more or less facing outward discouraging any conversation. Their story was that they were planning to move to the coast with all the family and were here in advance to make the arrangements. They needed an excuse in case of questions by police, at checkpoints, or just by curious even if friendly people.

The sun was quite low in the sky as they arrived at the square where they were to get off. A red-yellow orb just hanging there in the mist, the young and bleary firmament of the morning, and below it, people clothed in their various garbs, robes, and chilabas slowly drifting around, women and men and boys of all sizes and descriptions. Jamal mused, wondering who they all were and how many had been raped or used as he was to be. It was not an idle thought, but rather an anger, dismay that was building deep inside him. He did not understand this feeling, perhaps psychologists would have named it a form of PTSD, but as a young man who had been nurtured with such love by his mother and family and who was very devout and close to Allah, Jamaal had decided to interpret all that was happening to him and his final response as his own personal Jihad, his struggle, his sacrifice in the name of Allah, and to dedicate it all to Him.

The hotel was a hovel set above a smoky shop that sold bread and a local style of pizzas, a lump of dough kneaded, shaped, and loaded with cheese and tomato and all sorts, but then sanitised in the cleansing fire of the wood oven. Next door stood a dilapidated building that served as a tearoom with a front terrace teeming with white-jacketed waiters and patrons. Jamal felt quite at home in the hullabaloo, in the thought that nobody would know or care about him or what he was about to do. For a moment he was freed from his devils, until out of the corner of his eye he saw his uncle talking to someone. He saw a tall dark man who despite being an outsider seemed to merge successfully into the place, with his chilaba and hood half covering his face. His uncle returned to the table.

"We will go to the room now, Jamaal. You will wash with this soap, all of your body, your hair, all of you, and then you will put on the new clothes we brought for you."

"I don't feel like this pizza any longer." Suddenly he was nervous again. He realised that despite his thinking and praying and his resolutions, nothing had changed. Tears welled up in his eyes. His uncle took him discreetly by the arm, holding their meagre bags and belongings with the other, and led him with a fierce grip to the dark passage.

"Don't you go trying to change your mind now, killing your mother."

The boy was unable to speak. It was all so unfair and so monstrous, and his uncle was over- eager for him to become the willing pet of the other man.

"I will do it, but I will never forget this day, Kader, never," he said, now angry.

This was my meeting with Jamal.

"Come in, come in. Here, sit on the bed. You are trembling? Please do not be afraid. I will be gentle with you. I will not hurt you. Let me see you, look at me. You are so beautiful." He took the boy's face and held it in his hands, looking into his eyes. "Oh Ishmael, I have waited so long."

The boy smiled for him, not wanting to correct him. The man was so different. He smelt clean and good, his suit under the chilaba which he had cast off was smart and expensive looking. Jamaal smiled, recalling conversations with other boys: "Well if it has to be, better he be rich and good-looking."

Then the man asked him to stand in front of him and, looking up at the boy, he inserted his right hand under the boy's pants to find his full buttocks. As he gently fingered the boy's tiny anus, Jamal began to feel the excitement. The man pulled the boy's pants off completely.

"You are so incredibly beautiful." Gently he parted the boy's buttocks and inserted his tongue briefly into his anus. The man softly pulled the boy to the bed. He encircled him with his arm and began to kiss his mouth. The boy surrendered at once and found himself kissing the man back. The boy's hand went down as if of its own volition to seek out and weigh the man's penis in his hand.

"It's so big," he whispered, and the man smilingly guided the boy's head and mouth down. "Put it in your mouth and suck it."

The boy closed his eyes and worried about the size of the thing soon to enter his bottom. He thought he would do his best to empty the man first and then he would have no need to sodomise him. As the boy worked on his penis, the man went down to find the boy's small testicles which he gently put into his mouth one at a time and then cast his attention to his small, wonderfully formed instrument. It was not erect.

"Oh God, what have I done?" The man was holding his head in his hands and rolling as if bitten by a rabid dog. "Allah look down on me – I am evil. I have begun to commit an abomination with this boy." He began reciting the Surahs for the expiation of grievous sins.

The boy sat up abruptly, very afraid. "I am sorry, I am sorry," he whispered, terrorised, his tears welling up again.

"No." The man swept the boy up in his arms with a bearlike hug. "No, I am the sinner and have wanted to corrupt you as well. What we have been doing is one of the most beautiful of acts if performed with love and by two willing partners. We do not love each other. I love Ismael, who I would condemn to a vile death if I were to consummate my love for him with him, and so I scoured the internet for years to find someone worthy to be his substitute, and you have been coerced into it by your uncle and by your love for your sick mother. You must remember that an act of love between two people is always blessed. The problem is that I started this hoping that in some unthought-of way, it would be Ismael I was loving. Your uncle is a weak and unpleasant man, and you should not trust him."

Together they knelt, and the boy knew at that moment that Allah had intervened for him in answer to his prayers. They spoke at length for the rest of the day and into the night, taking water and nourishment at intervals, and praying. The man told him of what the assassin in Spain had done, of how he had killed a powerful and evil man, and that some of us would be called by God to do the same. The ones called, who carry out such an act will be called Ansaki, and must never be suspected or found out, must carry the secret for the rest of their lives.

Jamaal went to his uncle with the rest of the money that the man had given him but omitted to tell him that he had given a further five hundred American. They crept out of the hovel in which they had passed the night and in which rooms Jaamal's tussle with his devils had taken place. The money that Kader carried in his money belt turned him into a nervous wreck in the sure knowledge that they would be attacked for it.

"Don't act so furtively, you fool," Jamaal admonished him, much to the surprise and momentary irritation of the older man. But he was quiet because of the new authority in the boy. Perhaps he has truly been touched by the lord?

The red-yellow orb was just rising on the distant washes of a partially hidden sea, casting a weak misty light over the square. Snarling dogs and awakening beggars, the occasional figure on its way clothed heavily in its thick woollen chilaba despite the impending heat of the day. Buses coming and going. They waved one down and clambered aboard, Jamaal awkwardly feeling the lump tied to his inside leg, his hidden five hundred dollars, his family's passport to a new life. As they stood waiting for seats, a hand caressed him, and Jamal lashed out, a Jamal freed by

Allah from the devil that had wanted to pollute his spirit and seeking to protect his family's future.

"Cursed is he who does as the people of Lot did. He caressed my leg, my buttock." The other men started to push the miscreant off the bus, but Jamaal stopped them. "We are sorry," they said, "where do you come from?" Kader looked at his nephew blankly, and the boy responded in a powerful voice.

"We just need a small spot to continue with our prayers. There is only one God." He spoke loudly and the bus responded, "And Mohammed is his prophet."

Again they traveled through the burning desert. Jamaal would not eat or drink, he had made a promise. Some fellow travelers solicitously chastened him across his uncle's bulk saying that he would lose consciousness, so he gave in and drank. Before, men had loved him because he was beautiful and they desired him, but the boy noticed the change in that now they loved him because they felt that he was touched by the hand of Allah, and Allah had given him great beauty. So he made the promise at that moment to live for God.

"Jamaal, Jamaal, where have you been?" They had been giving her shots for days now and her recovery was instantaneous. "Where did you go with your father, Jamaal? Jamaal what have you done?"

Jamal and his father went to find Kader and his friend and retrieve the money they had taken for themselves. Kader they forgave as a brother after a good beating, and the shopkeeper they killed. Later, a note written in a very rudimentary hand was found in a mosque's charity box claiming the sanitation, the death by knife. The author of the sanitation claimed to be Ansaki, and the justification was the elimination of traffickers in young people and children. Copies of the note were posted in mosques by indignant members of the faithful all over the region, and a copy was sent to the office of the local press wire services.

Ismael

I noticed the attention that a certain high-ranking officer in a certain secret police body had begun to pay to the boy. Ismael worked in a public place, and this man, a man with a family and highly regarded in the local mosque, would visit this place frequently. At the start I paid scant attention and did nothing. After all, it was very difficult.

The man's work was to liaise with certain high-ranking government officials from America and other places, whom it was vaguely suspected were plotting covert operations to overthrow uncooperative governments. One such visitor, I later learned was also a congressman. It appears that the congressman took a shine to the beautiful boy, and a few days later Ismael disappeared. He had been arrested on charges of being an "enemy of the state", one of those vague instruments of law used by authoritarian regimes to subvert natural justice.

I went crazy. Since I had rejected the stand-in boy, Jamaal, my love for Ismael had become more intense than ever. I was a full-blooded homosexual male who had needed to live every moment of his life, waking or sleeping, hiding his true nature in the sure knowledge that any hint of the truth could lead to his execution by hanging, and public humiliation.

There was nothing I could do, only try as well as possible to tie up the loose ends when they found him, and get as close to the truth as possible. He was charged publicly with practising homosexuality and corrupting minors, and sentenced to be hung a few days later, but was shot when trying to escape. It broke my heart. I had loved the boy, in my own twisted yet pure way. Since my attempt to love him through another physical boy, my love for him had become a reality for me, a tangible thing. I know that the allegations of homosexuality were patently false; up to the moment of his kidnapping he had been pure as the driven snow, untouched.

At great expense and persistence, I finally came across a retired prison guard who had been employed in the house where he had been imprisoned. I kept my identity secret but was able to put together an idea of what went on. My health has greatly deteriorated as a result, and I prefer to allow the record to speak for itself if ever I have the chance to produce it as evidence. I can only say that the boy was abused, raped continuously, humiliated, and whipped often, and all at the whim of the American.

Thankfully, and what has led to my recovery, was the press release I had read before going to see Jamaal, and which I talked to him about at length the night we spent together. It was written by a person who calls himself Ansaki. I am now a participant in his chess game. My amputations, my Check Mates, have been, one American operative, come, congressman, and his liaisons in every single country, including the one here, that I have been able to discover. All the deaths were a matter of fact except for the American, Ismael's torturer. Him I left to the mercies of certain wild beasts of his own calibre. I am told that he took a long time to die. My press release has been prepared and released for the world to sit up and listen to. God is Great.

Chapter Eleven:
The Rooftop

"Hi Delai," Rocio muttered sweetly.

"We had arranged not to meet? I thought we were to be discreet."

"Yeah, but I saw your guy. I didn't want to send you any Wasap or make any phone calls so I thought it would be better if we just met."

"What guy, for heaven's sake?" Delai hissed. "The cops of half the world are out searching for us, and..."

They were sitting at a table on the massive sun terrace of a bar in Calahonda. It was a sultry September evening and the sun was still high in the sky, although it had lost its stifling daytime glare and heat. Some singers were just warming up and tuning their instruments for an evening gig.

"Rooftop something or other. Just go to the Zoco shopping centre and on the roof," she had said to Delai, who knew the place well but didn't let on. A young waiter sauntered over, smiled at them, and blushed at Delaisandra.

"Give us a minute, Sohail." He blushed again, smiled some more, and drifted off. "Sohail – that's a river?" she asked. "Named him after a river?"

"Yeah, in Fuengirola. Came from the Arabs, also a boy's name. In fact, for your further erudition, the name probably came first – the river may have been named for a person or simply for the meaning of the word. Why didn't you just come home, and anyway what guy?"

"I didn't come to your house coz I'm nervous. It's all gone haywire. This Ansaki guy's plan is working, working like shit! It's working, working! Do you know what happens to me when I get nervous, Delai?

"Don`t say that word so loudly, in fact, don't say it. What does happen to you? Do you get hungry? You want a whole goddam Edam cheese to eat, is that right?"

Rocio fixed her gaze on the other girl.

"Call Sohail, Delai. We both need a drink," she growled.

They managed to attract the boy's attention again. He smiled his way over. "That's what Sohail means – beautiful."

Rocio ordered two Camparis with blackcurrant cordial, and a bottle of champagne made in Cataluña.

"Early bingeing?" asked Delai with a grimace.

"Ain't he lovely?" said Rocio, scrutinising the boy intensely and unabashedly so that he blushed again and scuttled off as soon as he could.

"He'd do, to begin with," she said with a grin. "That's what I get hungry for. Or for you, Delai, although the competition would be a bit stiff."

"What are you on about? You're quite enigmatic today. What competition, and what guy?"

"That's what I've been trying to tell you, Delai. I saw him in Estepona, your Attila the Hun type, the old hunk. And I followed him, I stayed with him and his motorbike into the hills. I never knew it was so mountainous up there and deserted, only wild boar, you can tell from the grass, and Hispanic goats. And I've only just realised that he followed me back down. He's here – I saw him out of the corner of my eye as I came up the steps."

"Let's get out of here." The other girl leapt up and dragging Rocio by the hand ran out of the rear garden exit.

"Back in a minute," she signalled to a bemused Sohail, who was just approaching their table with a full tray. They ran down the steps, laughing at the ridiculous train of events Rocio had set in motion with her ill-timed amateur detective disaster.

"*Cabrona*, bitch," laughed Delai. "I don't even know if I want to meet him, and anyway he might just be mixed up in all of this, this unmentionable name, affair."

"You mean Ansaki?" stuttered the other girl in a shouted whisper.

"Oh my God, is she for real?" The Cuban girl threw her hands up to her head. They emerged from the narrow passageway and crossed the road.

"We'll take my car," she said. "Get yours later, Rocio."

Suddenly there was a massive crash and people screamed. Delai saw big men, a grey van with a door swung back unnaturally– that was the crash they had heard. She saw

Attilla going like nothing she had ever seen. It was just him and at least four big men trying to hit him. She raced back across the road, without thinking, and kicked a guy in the gut, a guy who was swinging what looked like an iron pipe at the back of the giant's head. He went down clutching his testicles and squealing. Attila turned with an armlock on one of his unhappy assailants and kicked out at another, smiling at her. He reached over, ripping what was left of the door off its hinges, and smashed it into another two of the gang. People were running down from the rooftop and other establishments – the racket was drawing the crowds. The unknown men, well bloodied now, were either lying inert on the ground or had disappeared, abandoning their van and friends to their fate.

Delai saw Sohail in the crowd. His face was unreadable. He's afraid, she thought. How strange. Then it occurred to her – so what did he come down for? He's meant to be waiting on tables in the rooftop? And then it dawned on her like a flash. He's one of them.

The big man paused and wiped his forehead. His assailants had all disappeared. He held out his hand to Delai as if they were meeting for afternoon tea. "Lots of irritating insects buzzing around these days. Thanks for your help – quite a rugger kick. I'm Pete. Let's get out of here."

They ran, climbed into her car, and roared out of the place even as the sirens heralded the arrival of the Guardia Civil.

"*Krav maga*," said Rocio sitting in the back, and said it again when no one answered. "Why did you follow me?" he asked curtly.

"I apologise for that," said Delai. "You can't choose all of your friend's idiosyncrasies these days, and Rocio is sometimes spontaneous to the point of being immature, but she's a good guy."

"Stop the car, please," he ordered sourly, and as the vehicle came to a stop he whirled around to face Rocio. "You stupid fuck," he snarled. "Those days have gone. You don't follow very large men who look like I do to lonely destinations. You're not dead now, lying in a shallow grave, because I don't do that sort of thing anymore. And it's *Gochinkwai*, fight to kill, as part of a whole potpourri of combat forms."

He hauled himself out of the car with a catlike ability unusual for a man of his size and weight. As he started back towards the shopping complex Delai hooted, and he stopped by her open window. "I don't know if it's important," she said, "but the waiter in the rooftop, the very nice- looking boy named Sohail, is into it. I saw it written on his face. He probably called them."

"Thank you," he said, "and for joining the fray on my behalf." He handed her a card with a number written on it. "Please send me a Wasap and your location," and with a brief thumbs up he set off again.

Pete retrieved his bike and settled down for a meal in a small bar across the road from the rooftop's car park. It was a nice location, Calahonda, close to the beach, and due to its hosting a better-heeled sort of visitor year in and year out, the area was well maintained with grassy lawns and recently tarmacked roads. He waited. He knew who the young guy Sohail was. He was the kind of boy who spotted men like Pete from a distance and made a beeline for them.

The food was good, sort of upmarket for a bar, with some interesting bits and snacks, so that Pete was able to pass the time.

"I was hoping to have a drink and listen to some music later. What time is that rooftop open till?" he asked.

"No, they close at midnight and it's nearly that now. Better you go up the road or stay here – all their crowd comes over to us once it closes."

Pete sat outside and waited till he saw the workers and drinkers, just five or six of them, approaching. As the young man passed his table, he reached out easily and took his wrist.

"Come sit with me, Sohail."

The others just continued into the bar, and the young guy allowed himself to be pulled gently until he turned his head and saw it was Pete. He was so petrified that he just went along silently.

"Let's go down the beach. I want to talk to you, boy," he said gruffly. Sohail just followed, dumbstruck with fear.

It was a warm night with a crescent moon that scarcely illuminated the sea and its gentle wavelets. Silhouetted against the dimly lit sea, a couple walked hand in hand and others played on the shore. Whispering and the occasional squeal or laugh told of the presence of lovers hidden under the nighttime darkness of the beach.

Pete could feel the cold night sand between his toes. He felt sorry for the boy, who was shaking like a leaf, but he needed to know what was going down. He lay on the sand in a secluded spot and pulled the now violently trembling boy down with him.

"Don't worry, I won't hurt you. Now tell me about it," Pete demanded.

"They came to the bar, left your photo, and gave me some money. Said you were living in the area and they needed to see you. Said I was to call them, so when you came I did. I didn't know they were going to attack you." He was sobbing now.

"Who are they?"

"I don't know," he sobbed.

"Look, boy, Sohail is your name? So Sohail, believe me when I tell you that you chose the wrong friends, and enemies if that is what you are trying to make of me. You set me up to be murdered."

"No, no, I'm sorry, I'm sorry, I didn't know. Now I'm locked between you and them and I'm so scared. I don't know what to do."

Pete pulled a clean tissue from a pack and gently cleaned the boy's face, calming him.

"They're from the Middle East. I know because I knew a family once from Israel and they speak the same." Then he hesitated. Pete ruffled his hair.

"Don't stop now. Let it out."

"I've been to their house. One of them likes me, you know, but I've only had drinks, smoked some weed with him, and talked in his bedroom. Talked about me mainly. He was interested."

"Ok, take me there." "But will they see me?"

"No, no way they will, and after you show me their place I will take you to your home where you can have an early night. I'm sure your mum will be surprised. And you can take down my number. From now on you Wasap me on anything, ok?"

Later Pete drove up to the location Delai had sent him. Spotting a car with someone in it parked directly opposite Delai's, he roared right up to it on his Harley, blinding the inmate with the glare of his headlight. The car started up and drove off.

"Who would have been a youngish guy, maybe 25 to 30, sitting in an old Merc parked across the road from your gate?"

"No idea. There are a whole bunch of Rumanians hang around in the area. During the crisis years, they would rip off everything in abandoned building sites, and it seems they never left. I shouldn't worry, though. We have our security team," she laughed. Pete's entrance through the gate set off a cacophony of barking.

"Yes, I know them," he said. "In the past, we used them as attack dogs." She glanced at him as if expecting more.

"Better we allow the past to remain where it is," he laughed. "Did you find out anything about the thugs with the grey van?"

"Secret service detachment from the Middle East democracy, probably here to teach the Spaniards how to suck eggs. Headed up by a particularly nasty bit of work named Ruben. Sohail took me to their house and I waited till I saw this guy and, well, that tells me all I need to know. I'll just let it ride for a while. Probably interested in me as their potential assassin suspect."

"Why should they be interested?" asked Delai

"Simply because the murdered Senator was a backer of Israel's annual subsidy from the US. We're talking three point eight billion per annum that Israel receives every year to assist them in their genocidal repression of the Palestinian people, and to act as the US strongman in the ME, bombing everyone every now and again as a reminder."

Early next morning at the rooftop:

"I just want some coffee for now, Sohail. My, you're up early today."

"He took me home early and sent me to bed, so I've come in so I can be free later." "Who did, Sohail?"

"He did. He's so scary and so strong and so beautiful, he'll probably destroy me when the moment comes. He took me down to the beach and pulled me on to him. I was so horny I was already feeling him inside me"

"If you're talking about Pete, then I very much doubt that the moment will ever come. He's all man and a gent at that."

"Well, he's my man. He said he'd look out for me," said the boy petulantly, stamping his foot. "Who put it into your head that you would be a man's boy?"

"Well," he said coyly, colouring slightly. "Don't tell anyone. We watch porn, me and my friends, and as there are no nice girls that I know, they all form groups together. I am not too big, in either way, so they said I could be a bottom. Well, I'm a virgin anyway, never been with anyone, well only a couple of masturbations here and there. And then Pete came along, and I like him, I love him."

Delai laughed and put her arm around the boy's shoulders.

"If he said he'll look out for you, that means he's going to be your friend, and I'll help as well. See if I can find some pretty little Arab girl to introduce you to. You don't need to do anything, just get to know her, become friends."

"Ok," he smiled. "Anyway, it's the Spanish boys who try these things. We Muslims have it deep down inside us that it's not right, not truly natural. Some Muslim boys I know will do it, but just the active part for money. Anyway, if our parents suspect anything they marry us off quickly."

114

Suddenly the boy blushed and Delai spun around in her seat. Pete took the empty bench and maneuvered himself to face her and the boy.

"Listen to me carefully, both of you. We have a small problem. Sohail, now don't be alarmed, it's only routine. The police will arrive here at any minute and arrest you." The boy went pale. "Don't worry," said Pete. "They'll also arrest me. Now listen, boy, there's no problem, and I am with you. The police know me, but they need to go through the motions. They will ask you all about the house of those men and the time you went there, and you will tell them everything, the truth, about the fight and how I made you take me there later."

"What happened?" hissed Delai.

"They topped him, killed the vermin, Ruben Misrahi. He had it coming – been killing children for years, most recently in Palestine where he's a colonel in the IOF. This will probably open the floodgates, and there will be a spate of such, accidents, wherever these animals are to be found. He was a specialist in shooting them or having them shot in the stomach and then getting his Mickey Mouse troops to stop any ambulance from getting through so the kid would bleed to death."

They came in silently and unobtrusively, three dark-suited individuals. Heads immediately began to turn, and after the suits some half a dozen uniformed Policia National.

"Hello, Pete. I trust you remember me. I am Juan Betardo, here now in my capacity as Inspector Jefe of the Judicial

Brigade of the National Police. I have come personally because of our old friendship, and because we are aware of your diplomatic status. As such I would extend my invitation to accompany us."

"What about the boy, Juan?" asked Pete. The chief inspector looked long and amusedly at him. "Perhaps your tastes have changed, my friend?"

"Perhaps hell will freeze over," growled Pete. "Treat him right, he's a good kid. Could be my son."

"Sure, Pete, we won't arrest him, just invite him along for questioning and tea at the station." "Sohail, that is your name as shown here on your ID card?"

"Yes sir."

"Would you like to come with us to help us with our inquiries?" "Yes sir. I want to go with Mr Pete,"

"I think that's a new one for your *mosquerío*, Pete. He's adopted you." (*Mosquerío* is the cloud of insects that accompany a *burro*, hovering around its head.)

The chief inspector bowed formally to Delai. "*Señorita, a sus pies.*" (Young lady, I am at your feet.) He spun on his heels, and the whole convoy moved out in unison.

"Shit," mused Delai. "There are still some gentlemen left in Spain."

Chapter Twelve:
Ansaki Second Press Release

Some time back I killed an American senator, an evil man, and a perturbation to world peace, democracy, justice, and security. I thank God that today the world is a better place due to this man's absence. It seems however that those who surrounded him and helped him hold together his ill deeds have not desisted, so that they are in all probability attracting the attention of other Ansaki.

Today I have killed a second man, an evil man, a creature of darkness.

"A spirit passed me by, the hair of my flesh stood on end and made me shudder with fear."

Today this demon is no more. This man was an evil killer in the east of Europe, always successfully stationing himself in the ideal place to be able to find undefended children to prey upon and finally destroy to satisfy his evil lusts. I followed his grisly footsteps from afar for many years until at last, he arrived in the so-called Middle Eastern democratic enclave, a holding of lands and cities stolen from the people of Palestine. Here this man ascended to the rank of colonel in the occupation forces. He was one of the many responsible for the untimely deaths of so many innocent Palestinian people, and so many children. His specialty was to shoot a child in the stomach, for the mere crime of participating in a demonstration against the

117

destruction of their villages, and as the child lay agonising on the dusty floor losing its lifeblood, he would stop the Palestinian ambulances from being able to approach and assist the child. After some time under the blazing sun, the child would die and the noble occupiers would add another notch to their diabolical record of child murder.

As an observer of the Palestinian genocide by the Middle Eastern democracy and America, I have seen comprehensive lists, freely available on the internet, a list of the atrocities committed, just in the last 22 years. It's a list of evil. Such a list is published by Amnesty International amongst others. Please check it out, investigate it, and understand the level of evil being practiced and the amount of Ansaki attention it deserves.

I am grateful to God that new Ansaki are appearing in so many corners of the globe but will point out that they are a drop in the ocean compared to the need for evil doers to realise that either they cease or will be stopped from further hurting humanity. I will identify those áreas which in my very humble opinion most desperately require study by Ansaki all around the world.

The fossil fuels industry worldwide, including all those involved, politically, financially, and in any way. This industry if allowed to continue its rampage unhampered will be one of the main factors leading to the destruction of our planet. It appears that many in power glibly assume that *later* they will be able to reverse the damage once the poorest two-thirds of the earth's population has been wiped out.

Corrupt politicians who mislead, lie, and act to the detriment of their voters and the public at large. As politicians have the job of exercising their votes and decisions and influence to support a point of view, any Ansaki research on a specific politician should be intense and thorough. In other words, it must be seen over the years that the politician in question was proceeding in a way that constitutes a definitive evil.

Persons, and I say persons because all sorts have jumped onto the bandwagon of distorting and disrupting the normal functioning of the minds of young and older children. All those who are involved for the sake of personal profit or gain in the manipulation of the minds of children seeking to mess with their mental or physical integrity should also fall under the scrutiny of those Ansaki qualified to understand what is happening.

Those involved in the planning and implementation of new taboos and tendencies that are detrimental to humanity at large and designed for the greater power of certain sectors within our societies, and the finality of profit, will also fall foul of those Ansaki aware of their actions.

Businesspeople of any sort or definition (Including bankers and banking operatives and financial dealers of any sort) who cheat, distort, mislead, and in so doing lead to the downfall and destruction of families and individuals.

All those be they politicians, opportunist profiteers, bankers, or other such who have been and are instrumental in the despoiling of essential services in any country in the world, a good example being the freshwater supplies of a powerful island state close to France, where illegal practices and theft have led to the loss of billions by the people and the sewage infection of their rivers and seas.

Ansaki hunters. Whereas it is understood that police forces in furtherance of their continuing duty will investigate all crimes including Ansaki sanitations, Ansaki will target all bodies and individuals that seek to destroy them and the concept, be they secret services of any nation, or special task forces set up for the pursuit and destruction of the Ansaki concept.

I would clarify that when I make this list I am not speaking purely of the West. In the West, we are so much more aware of the faults of powerful people because we are still ostensibly a democratic block despite the abuses being committed so shockingly these days against the press, freedom of speech, and other of our civil liberties. The investigations of evil and sanitations should happen everywhere on God's earth.

Corporations: all those that favour the breaking of anti-trust laws and defy monopoly restrictions. All of those who create or continue to produce anything detrimental to the well- being of the planet or its inhabitants.

Judges and legal agents, including police, of all sorts who distort the law evilly for their own profit to the detriment of the innocent. Priests, chaplains, pastors, Imans, and religious leaders who willfully lie and distort the truth for profit and to the detriment of their faithful and others.

Secret organisations disguised as NGOs or however hidden, whose function is to fund every sort of dissent or possible upheaval in countries all around the world. It's a known fact, to give you just the tip of a massive iceberg, that the following revolutions were powered from countries outside the frontiers of where the subversion occurred:

Arab Dawn, Libya, Syria, Ukraine, Somalia, Mali, Sudan. Yemen, Afghanistan, Iraq, Yugoslavia, Haiti, Iran, the list goes on and on You name it. These are just place names to us here in the West, whereas, in fact, they are places where people live, where innocent little children go to school each day.

And of course FAKE NEWS, all those who create fake news with evil intentions in mind as also those who prevent the world from knowing the truth.

We will create chaos, many will say, but no chaos is more terrible or evil than that which we suffer today. When our children in the West eat plastic each day, and where a huge part of the world's children and population eat nothing at all. Where bullies, be they states or people, create havoc killing millions for profit, ride rampant. And yet we in the West go with our families to the beach and all is rosy, but it's not. For millions today, and even for us in the not- so-distant future, hell is looming.

"Delai, it's me, Rocio. Are you in?" She was standing at the gate to Delai's grandad's house, shouting into the street intercom. It was a blowy day with slightly overcast skies. The wind tore along the road on which the house stood amongst unfinished housing developments on an urbanisation built on the upper end of the motorway at Riviera in Mijas Costa. She got no reply, but the buzzer went so she opened the gate and cautiously poked her head around it to check that the dogs had been locked away from the entrance area.

The house door swung open.

"Come in Rocio, come in. I was just about to call you. This telepathy does work you know – we should chuck our phones and become a telepathic phenomenon."

"He's not here, is he?"

Delai grinned widely. "No, of course, he's not. Last I saw of him he was carried off for questioning by the police, and not any police, no sir, the Inspector Jefe himself. Apparently, Pete and he are old comrades or something."

"It's all getting quite heavy, Delai."

"It's nothing to do with us, silly. It's about the shooting of that… Oh, you don't know. Well, the leader of those guys who attacked Pete was shot dead last night, so Pete and his new lover from afar have been taken."

"Shot dead? Here? Delai, shit. All of this is beginning to make me very nervous. And I thought he'd be doing you by now."

Delai burst out laughing,

"What, Pete? I believe in true love, silly! You *niñas* (girls) in Spain may think it's wonderful just dropping your panties at the first *venga(let's go)*, but true love beats it all, and the guy is incredible. Now Sohail, you know, the pretty waiter, well he's a secret virgin, all the guys he hangs with have convinced him he's gay, and he now reckons he wants Pete to be his first man, his deflowerer."

"So Pete is gay?" screeched Rocio.

"No, of course, he's not, he just told the boy that he would look out for him, and as the boy has this thing about being gay, he thinks that Pete is after his pretty bottom. But I have put paid to all that nonsense. I've told Sohail that I would find him a sweet little thing, a girl to fall for, so next time we see him he'll be acting all macho."

"Would I do?" asked Rocio smoothing back her hair.

"Do for what?"

"Could I be the pretty little thing?" "But you're gay."

"Well, there's gay and there's stupid."

"You're not exactly what I had in mind, but it's a free country. Only watch out for his new protector." Rocio gazed at her in a gormless inquisition. "Pete, of course!"

"So why were you going to call me," asked Rocio coyly, only to have her face drop when Delai told her of the new press release. "Should we just burn it and pretend we know nothing?"

"Come on Rocio, for heaven's sake, look at Julian Assange. Take a page from his book, he's a true hero for the people and for truth, and truth is what it's all about. Look why should this person not be heard by the world? Anyway, he rings true. The world is being destroyed by a bunch of murderers. But we don't have to agree or disagree – we are just publishers."

"So was Assange," said Rocio in a quiet voice. "But I suppose we can't let this murderer down, though. Robin Hood was a murderer. Ok, let's go for it, but now I must seduce that little virgin waiter. If I am going to be locked away for years, I need a good seeing to before I go."

They sat quietly for a while as they read and digested the content of the new missive.

"So it was him again? This killing was last night the man was the guy Pete is being questioned about."

"The police will soon know that Pete had nothing to do with it said Delai.

I feel privileged that God has seen fit to give me the opportunity to be the purveyor of such a matter to the people of the world. Be his message right or wrong it must be seen it must be heard, and the people themselves can judge, and not the animals who currently hold sway over the lives of all on the planet. And I will go one further, I will become an Ansaki in my own way. I am coming across quite a few Ansaki confessions on social media, although they rarely last five minutes, as well as mailings and squeaks in alternative newspapers. I am going to make it my job to compile as many as I can and publicise them so that the world becomes aware of what is truly happening. So that the Ansaki concept grows and gains new adepts and becomes the world conscience.

ANSAKI DEVOUT

Chapter Thirteen:
Police Barracks

The assault by Franco's rebel troops and the Italian divisions signalled the worse of the Civil War in Malaga in February of 1937. Families gathered what belongings they could and made for the Almeria road as massive shelling destroyed thousands of buildings. La Desbanda was to be remembered as the most numerous exodus of the war, and the greatest atrocity imposed upon a civilian population by the fascists. Queipo de Llano, the fascist general who had prided himself on inciting his legions and regulares to rape and murder the civilian population, had successfully created a terror so great that 150,000 human beings fled along the Almeria road. Queipo de Llano sent warships to fire upon the fleeing people, along with the German Condor squadron and the Italians. Eight thousand innocents were slaughtered, and civilians and families were murdered.

Throughout his life, his grandmother, Maria had told him stories. But there was one in particular that Juan Betardo would never forget.

"I saw a man whose face was bleeding and he was walking, then we found a dead woman with no legs and a boy who was crying, and he followed us. We could hear the thunder that my mother said was the warships firing their guns. Then suddenly the planes came and my father pushed the boy and me onto the rocks, and I cried as I cut my leg. The planes shot at my mother, and as my father tried to get her they shot him as well. The boy was your grandfather, Jose Betardo Garcia."

Juan Betardo the policeman never forgot what his origins were, and where he came from.

For years into the Seventies and Eighties, the area all around where the new police barracks was eventually constructed continued to be a mass of windowless, roofless, destroyed residential properties, sprawling for kilometres. People did live there for a while, until the new regime started constructing huge buildings in the newly planned residential zones on the outskirts, and the slums were deserted.

The barracks of the Policia Nacional is a large purpose-built edifice situated right at the main motorway turnoff heading towards the centre of the capital. Just up the four-lane highway is El Corte Ingles and then the black Hacienda(Tax Authority) building. The bridge, with lane-wide pavements on either side, carries the whole highway over the dry riverbed of the Guadalmedina and into the start of the old Alameda, Malaga's central and historic thoroughfare.

The specially constructed *Sala de exposiciones* in the barracks of the Policia Nacional of Malaga is a large auditorium accommodating some hundred and fifty persons, comfortably ensconced in cinema-style seating. At the front of the place is a raised wooden dais that runs the whole width of the hall. The dais is partially occupied by a long set of tables covered with a baize cloth at which sit the speakers. The boards behind the speakers have been replaced by the specially deployed US technicians with three very large screens or banks of smaller screens.

The mainly female chatter is incessant, charming, and amusing, the air is lit up by it, and yet accompanying this wonderful Spanish attitude is the massive workload carried by the perhaps twenty operators, mainly girls, all uniformed in the smart attire of the police, yet with that dress style that is one of the most giveaway clues to their national identity. They are busy feeding the computers and monitors that sit on the desks with up-to-the-minute information that is to appear on the screens. They belong mainly to the team of profilers flown in from Madrid and are accommodated in an ample L-shaped section near the entrance to the hall. The monitor screens and consoles they are working at are connected by a sizeable WI-Fi system to a barrage of computers below the screens.

Their leader, Laura Galvez Diaz, is a tough lady of some fifty years of age who has made the grade as a chief inspector and is very highly regarded in the Policia Nacional due to her dogged persistence, intelligence, and natural ability in her work as a profiler. She is a psychological criminologist, so her field of knowledge and expertise touches upon all the fields and sciences which go to make up criminology.

"I am Dr Laura Galvez, and I will be working with you all in my capacity as profiler. Call me Laura — I only mention my doctorate so you will understand that I am qualified to work hand in hand with my expert colleagues in their own fields. In particular, the forensic psychologist, whose job will be to validate all our conclusions before the coroner and in all fields legal. "I and my team are part of the task force headed by Chief Inspector Juan Betardo of the National Police and his colleague Jose Garcia of the Guardia Civil, both of whom are seated here with me on the dais.

Chief Inspector Betardo is known for preferring to hide his light under a bushel, which has left me with the task of bringing things into some sort of perspective. My team and I have been heavily involved since the unfortunate incident took place, in conjunction with our colleagues in forensics, ballistics, bloodstain pattern analysis, DNA fingerprinting, and fingerprinting, in coordinating and recording all the forensic information we are fed with. As you are aware, the crime scene, and we are talking about the whole crime scene, has been frozen since the incident, accessed only in accordance with existing protocols by qualified members of this investigation."

"So what specific suspects do we have in custody, Laura? The weeks are flying past and it all seems to be weekends and mañanas." A big man seated at the front spoke through his mike. "I'm Jim Levin, SBI."

"Yes, Jim, you are working with us daily, so?" She faltered. "The weeks do go by and we are doing everything. As you know, it's a process, and we have analysed the available films of the accesses to the motorway from Sotogrande during one hour on either side of the time of the shooting.

Our work has been made much more difficult by the passing of the motorbike concentration involving thousands of individuals by Sotogrande at that moment."

"Thank you, Laura, that was just for the record and for Matt here, who has just flown in. I'll also throw in my 'racist' request. I have suggested that to expedite matters we start with just the Arabs and Muslims, and any Iranians."

"And I will again advise you that that would be contrary to European Law. Here in this country, we cannot discriminate based on race religion, gender, or colour. The law quite specifically states that protected characteristics can never be the sole basis for profiling. But let me point out, special agent, that in your country the success rate is predominantly with serial killers and is due to the re-emergence of the criminal. Our criminal in this case is presumably a cleanskin and promises to be a one-off offender, thereby depriving us of the easy path to the success enjoyed in the US."

"May I respectfully point out that this is now a major international problem, Laura, and whatever we can do to speed the process along..."

"Yes, Special Agent, but not at the expense of our rule of law and our democracy, otherwise we will have nothing."

"May I say a few words here, Laura." The Chief Inspector raised his hand as if in school. "Jim, colleagues, ladies, and gentlemen. Let's have a look at the list of possible suspects." The three screens were suddenly filled with hundreds of names, and a sound of amazement rose from the attending people.

"We've had a hard time trying to reach any useful conclusions from a forensic viewpoint. The shooter's vantage place, the lift, and the area surrounding it have been scrutinised layer by layer. If anything had been there we DNAed it. We fingerprinted it, we have followed every possible lead emanating from the whole crime scene, and our ballistics people, in spite of their efforts, have done little more than to put a specific definition on what we already knew, apart from identifying the weapon type so frequent and universal that it gives us nothing. It comes from a massive old issue that appeared in Europe after the war and is not registered anywhere. We know everything, we have been through that crime scene intensively, and at this moment what we need to do and are doing is look at the shooter and his or her victim. We have made repeated requests to you for all the available information on our victim, the deceased American Senator and the cooperation is 'Shy'."

"You know what they're like, Juan," put in Special Agent Levin. But Betardo carried ponderously on with his delivery.

"So our task now is to continue with, first of all, the algorithmic profiling. I say continue, decide to carry out all such profiling on our new murder as well. Anything that is done on the second murder will in no way interfere with or delay the physical interviewing and profiling already being carried out extensively on our murder, that of the Senator.

"And may I say that there is at this time no evidence to link the two murders, and it would be a grave error to jump to any conclusions? However, that is down to Dr Laura Galvez, who will decide if and when the two crime scenes are to be triangulated. That is where similarities will be pinpointed, but we will do it graphically to inspire our thoughts."

The chief inspector grabbed a chair from behind the dais and sat on it from back to front, looking out at the gathering.

"Any press?" he asked. "No, " he answered himself. We are all professionals here, police, Guardia Civil. May I safely say that all technicians here belong to either body?" A grizzled, grey- haired man coughed politely into his mike.

"You may indeed, Jefe, but some of us, although closely affiliated to those bodies over the years, are independent professionals."

" All documentation was controlled at the entrance," assured Laura Galvez.

"Thank you, Laura. Ok, friends and colleagues, let's get down to business. What do we have here? We have a very careful and thorough criminal who has left no discernible trace anywhere on or around the crime scene. Our people have been busy on the streets all over the province and *nada*, nothing, at all. Then this press release, if it can be called such, appears in the media We are now anxious to interview the creators of this release, but are at a loss as to how to trace its origins. The authors are professionals and have known how to gain access to what is a highly restricted world press, without needing to disclose their identity, and we are still nowhere. And in all of this, we have had the assistance and cooperation of all the Western world's intelligence bodies, all of whom are as anxious as we are to lay this demon to rest. Did I say Western? No, it's most of the world that is concerned and willing to assist, because these Ansakis by definition intend to be a scourge wherever they identify an evil.

"So who is this killer? Let's identify the killer with a male gender for now as it's easier, and males are ten times more likely to commit a murder than are women. In a classical serial killing, the profiler would tend to anticipate that the killer acted in a psychopathological fashion, that he sees the whole scene repeatedly in his mind and links the different aspects to thoughts and emotions of his own. Thereafter those thoughts and emotions grow and pleasure him. The investigator has the task of deducing small idiosyncrasies of the killer's personality based on the crime scene.

"Time of day, light, access to the crime scene, noises, and environmental conditions. So we know that this was a physically fit, youngish man twenty to forty-five, with good eyesight. To what extent was this a planned hit? I would venture that the killer had the Senator in his sights from a long while back, that he knew of him by reputation, that he may even have studied his life and career. *But* this was a totally opportunistic hit, in my mind, which, given that it was so clean, makes this killer tremendously dangerous. He moves on his feet and in his mind with the greatest agility, calmly, intelligently, and at speed. How am I doing so far, Laura?"

"Very well, Chief Inspector. I would, of course, tend to seek a background issue, sexual, bullying, greed, or maybe fear as what moves him. After all, we are talking here of a cold-blooded killing, not a game of football."

"And the press release?" barked Betardo.

"To me, it means nothing. At this time, we don't even know if he wrote it."

"Well, I have read and read and re-read the release and, if it is a fabrication by a loon, it's a damned good one. I'll tell you all what I think. I know I have a reputation for the unorthodox, but it must be the bloodhound in me. At least I don't bay.

"The killer may indeed be tortured, but what by? Highly intelligent type. Perversion, yes, but not his. Where does all the money madness, the power lust, the perversion of all sorts come from? It comes from within man. The world we live in today, its perversion is contrary to the total concept of our Judaeo-Christian civilisation. He's spelling it out to us, and I for one am listening. The press release is a plea for sanity in an insane world, and it plots a course of action to counter that insanity.

"So, I began having a look at concluded profile descriptions, and a few took my attention."

The audience listened raptly now, as most of them were involved in the time-consuming slog of interviewing and profiling.

"Not all of those who took my eye at this moment have been interviewed and profiled. There is a group of five young men whose general body language and styles in the videos caught my eye. It transpires that they are three boys from the Rif Mountains of Morocco, a very conflictive region historically, and two lads from the mountains of Marrakech, another problem area."

"So you seem to be breaking the rules here, Juan?"

"Not at all, Jim. My interest was fired by the demeanour of the individuals, and not because they are Arabs. Their nationality and ethnicity have only come into play as a consequence. In other words, I did not specifically segregate these people for my interest.

"There was also this very big man. He has not yet been interviewed – his file, which I scanned cursorily, was one of the many to be processed. He holds a Russian diplomatic passport and also carries diplomatic letters from Algeria that claim diplomatic immunity for him. I know him from long ago, he is a good man and not involved, although I will be interviewing him re the new murder. He is here in the barracks as my guest. However, he was seen in the company, before the shooting, of three very dubious-looking types. He tells us they were Afghans whom he knew from before. Their files are also there, and I have asked for them to be located and invited, or encouraged, to come in.

"There is also a suspect who has just come to our attention, by accident, as it were. In my scanning of arrest and complaint reports for the last month, I tend to flip through these files in the way that manufacturers scan competitors' products, or farmers scan country magazines. Well, I scan occurrences. My attention is drawn by the unusual. So what more unusual than a young man from a good family who is extravagantly flamboyant in his reported dress sense – or undress, as he lately flung all his clothes into the sea at a much-frequented beach near La Cala de Mijas. He has a history of doing eccentric things but is never a real problem, just a bit of a shocker, an imaginative streaker type.

"He made his latest appearance in a product presentation show at a spa hotel in Benahavis where he took over the stage, and security had to be called as he was making all sorts of disparaging statements. Again, nothing serious, except that this guy is twenty-seven and a qualified doctor. For me, something is strange here. He actually finished his studies and is qualified, yet does not practice seriously. Yes, we are told he has done stints working with children with special needs, as well as children who have been the victims of accidents. We know very little about him so far, but in my book, he's our hottest potential suspect yet. After all, he left the hotel venue at Benahavis on his motorbike at about one am, turned up towards the hills and the canyon, and after that, we know nothing. So he certainly fits the bill for our shooter, although, even if he does fit my profile idea, I realise that to put a weapon in his hand and suspect him of the murder of a US Senator requires a good stretch of the imagination. So let's give him top priority. We need to know the ins and outs of a cat's behind with regard to him, his family, friends, and movements. The name is Alarico O'Donovan de Medinacheli. Get him up on the big screen, please."

Chapter Fourteen:
Doctor Alarico O'Donovan
de Medinacheli

It was eight in the morning, with an already aggressive sun beginning to cast its rays over the Mijas Mountains.

"Why just you and I, Juan? I would have thought a raid, a complete encirclement of the estate would have been more practical. You've always had an uncanny knack with this sort of thing, an intuition, or maybe you're just lucky, so to have jumped in with both feet may well have been the thing to do..."

"No, Jose, we're in the game now, the chase, remember. What do you want flatfooted police and Guardia running all around the place for? When we get up to this stage in an investigation we are like Quentin Tarantino and his mate Roberto Rodriguez. They always work together – regardless of who gets the film contract, the other is always invited along as a consultant."

"You're mad, Juan," the Guardia Civil captain chortled good-humouredly. Here, let's stop in at this *venta* for coffee. We can ask discreetly about the O'Donovan family as we eat our tostadas."

The *venta* was full of silent workmen. Some had coffee, and others brandy or brandy mixed with anis or beer. The two policemen looked at each other and shrugged as if to say,

"How can they, and so early." They sat at a window table and waited for the solitary and phlegmatic waiter to get to them.

"*Benemerita?*" he asked with a sly wink, "Guardia civil?" "Well," started up Juan...

"If you're not, I'll go to another table who were here before you, with respect." "No," said Jose. "I mean yes, I am, he's not."

"I can smell you guys out. I was right, so what can I get you, gentlemen? Although your friend is not off the hook yet."

"Ok! Ok!" laughed Juan. "Policia. Ok, now get us our coffee."

By the time they had been served and enjoyed their breakfasts of toast with oil and tomato, most of the workmen had left and the place was empty apart from a couple of stragglers enjoying their *Sol y Sombras* (anis with brandy) at the bar. The waiter slowly made his way back to their table.

"How do you cope?" asked Juan.

"I am fast," he said, looking straight at them deadpan. Then he smiled. "My nephew, he will come out now, he is fast, truly fast, makes me nervous he is so fast."

"Can you keep a secret? What is your name?"

"I am Elias, Sir. Yes, of course... If I can help the Benemerita, then dumb is the word."

"The family O'Donovan…" The policeman managed to get no further with his intended words.

"Good people. She was a saint, a nurse, died of cancer ten years ago. He changed, the man. Scottish. She was his life. When she went I think he also died. Now he's better, drinks wine, lots of good wine, comes with a young girl now and then, none of my business. I would do the same if I could. Nice young girls."

"Were there any children?" asked Jose.

"Yes, a boy, two boys, but one died young, six or seven, fell off his horse and broke his neck. The other boy, now in his twenties, went to study when his mother passed, became a doctor or something, and an uncle, one of her brothers, took him under his wing. But now he hangs around here, a devil for the women. A good-looking boy. Has a girlfriend of sorts, and comes in here with her and friends sometimes. Nice girl, very strange – my nephew says she's intense and gives him the creeps, although she is a looker.

"What are they suspected of? Now I surely am entitled to some answers. I am dumb, *Señores*, remember?"

"Yes, Elias, quite dumb, but you see we are not meant." He looked over at Jose. "What do you think, my friend?"

"I think we can rely on Elias." He went on, taking his colleague's lead. "Juan worries because we are after a big drugs haul and know that some of the operatives live or are lodged in this area."

"I don't see it," cut in Elias. "Not for the O'Donovan people. The boy is crazy, yes, and sometimes very strange, but very natural and clean, no drink nor drugs, just crazy, does things.

And the old man, no, never, he is not the type. Also, why would he? They are wealthy people. No, no, sorry but I think you received a bad *chivatazo*, tip-off. "

"What about the girlfriend, and the friends of the boy? Where could we find them?"

"Again, a very nice family. English mother, father *Mijeño*, from here, was a schoolteacher and she does things with computers. They live in that big red house opposite on the hillside. I will point it out to you, but please, they are a nice family."

"Don't worry," said Juan. "We will just go along and knock on the door and say we are checking on the O'Donovan boy because he does strange things in public. What do you think?" asked Juan. "Will they be ok with that?"

"Yes, yes," said the waiter. "Like that, you can talk about drugs and make it look like you are worried about the boy. They should make you an inspector, Juan. Together we could solve many cases."

"May we pay the bill, Elias, please, and if you would be so kind as to point out both houses we will be on our way," said Jose, standing up.

"Both houses? I will happily point out the girl's house and the direction to the O'Donovan finca, although I doubt you will find anyone there apart from a gardener and the dogs. At the O'Donovan's house that is. He will be out riding or walking; he is never there of a morning."

"And the boy?" "The boy is gone."

"Gone where?" they asked in chorus.

"I don't know the name, some funny place. Pepe! Pepe!" he called loudly. "My nephew Pepe he will know. He is bright, young." A clean-cut, attractive young man with a short haircut, slim and well-built, came out of the kitchen.

"What do you want, Elias?"

"Tell these friends where the O'Donovan boy has gone to."

"That Alarico, he's mad, crazy. I didn't think people were allowed to go there, it's so dangerous. He went to Gaza, the Gaza Strip. Well, he is a doctor. I suppose they need doctors with those Israeli murderers dropping bombs all the time. But no, he's mad. We live so well here, why should he want to go to Gaza?"

"To help others," said Juan in a quiet voice.

As they stood by their unmarked vehicle in the car park with Elias giving them directions to both houses, two Guardia Civil patrol cars drove in and parked, probably for breakfast. The officers walked over towards where they stood on their way to the entrance. As they saw the captain they began to stand to attention and salute, but Jose put his finger to his lips, and the officers relaxed immediately and walked past with a *"Buenos dias, señores."*

"I'm not stupid, you know. I saw that. They don't stand to attention for any Tom, Dick, or Harry, and it was all of them, not just one," said Elias.

"Well said, Juan. We don't know. Better you ask them. Maybe they were saluting you, Elias." Elias returned to the *venta* and accosted the Civiles.

"Who are those guys?"

"Better you don't ask," was the curt reply. They all ignored him and looked into their coffee. Elias went into his tiny office and called a number.

"Maria, tell the *señores* that some police and Guardia Civil are coming round." "What do they want? Nothing here for them."

"But tell them, Maria. You will not get rid of these just by pushing your chest out and protesting. These are high-ups. I have no idea what they want. They said it was about drugs, but they were asking about the O'Donovan boy and Sally Anne."

"No drugs here, but the O'Donovan boy, I'm not surprised. Ok, there's the gate now, it could be them. If they touch me or anything like that there'll be trouble, although it would be them who would get set upon by Mr. Harry and Miss Victoria. If there's any police brutality, I will call you, you can rush round and save the household."

She walked slowly and deliberately down the drive to the big double wrought-iron gates which gave access to the street, it was a large rustic house, with lots of wood and porches all around, set in some two hectares of land. As one approached it from the front gate and negotiated the drive it seemed to aspire to look like a mini-mansion.

She challenged the visitors at the gate.

"Que desean?" (What do you want?)

"Buenas tardes, Señora. Are you the lady of the house?"

"She is indisposed. Again, who are you and what do you want?"

"Madame, we are from the National Police. Please open the gate and allow us to enter, or call the lady or gentleman of the house."

"Que pasa, Maria? Quienes son los señores? Hahaha." A harmonious softly spoken but audible voice preceded its owner, who joined them at the gates. A small, wispy-haired, smiling, affable man who followed each phrase with a hahaha.

"Yes, gentlemen how may I help? Hahahaha."

"From the police, Sir," put in Juan. "Just a few words,"

"Of course. Maria, the dogs, please. This way gentlemen, do come in. Yes, the small one has an attitude towards authority, hahaha, and has been known to snarl, nip, and even bite, hahaha, no but not the police. No, not the police, no problem with them. No Sir, funny but it's only the Guardia Civil she hates, detests, hahaha. Strange the way she can spot the difference. Uncanny, hahaha, I'd call it."

"I am from the Guardia Civil," said Jose Garcia as they entered the house. "I will be sure to carry my statutory pistol next time I visit in case she detects my presence."

"We're here about the boy," said Juan, "the boy who runs around with your girl."

"Oh! Hahaha!" said the man. "I, by the way, am Roberto Diez Diez, hahaha, a retired school teacher, at your service, hahaha. And you gentlemen are?"

"I am Juan Betardo from the National Police and my colleague is Jose Garcia from the Guardia Civil."

"Yes," said the schoolteacher, "and what are you doing together, hahaha?"

"We ask the questions," said an irate Jose Garcia, somewhat nonplussed by the other's manner of speech.

"My apologies for my rather irritating speech defect, hahaha. It's not assumed, I can assure you, hahaha. No, please," he continued over Jose's apologetic protestations. "If ever you have Danish or some Swedish people as friends, hahaha, they gasp at the end of each phrase. Yet neither they nor their fellows are aware of it, hahaha. I personally am not aware either, but realise what happens, and so I can but say sorry. So please, what are you doing together? You see, hahaha, I have this antenna for incongruities, and neither of you look like or has the demeanor or presence of a beat policeman." The policemen looked at each other until Juan smiled.

"I am Chief Inspector Juan Betardo of the judicial branch of the National Police based in Malaga and responsible to Madrid, and Captain Jose Garcia is my counterpart in the Guardia Civil."

The little man looked stunned.

"I've read about you both in national and even European investigations. You are famous international sleuths, hahaha, top of the range. What then, what the f–k are you doing here? Forgive my Chinese, hahaha."

"The truth is," said Juan, "that we often tend to take certain aspects of certain cases and follow them ourselves. It's not following protocol, of course, but we generally enjoy a great deal of success. Meanwhile, the main drive is being run by a highly capable criminologist from the Malaga barracks."

"The main drive of what, for heaven's sake?" retorted the schoolteacher. "You make it sound like a search for a serial killer." Then it dawned on him and he went silent. "The boy?" he asked. "Impossible. I've more or less brought him up. He's always been around here. I've lived his brother's death, his mother's, his heartbreak, his uncle's, his studying to escape from himself," said Roberto. "No, no way. I've seen him in fights to defend animals. He wouldn't hurt a fly."

"Tell us about his relationship with your daughter."

"Well, what can I tell you? Both are highly intelligent and deep individuals. They seem to love each other as would a brother and sister. I don't know if they are actually a couple. He does seem to lead, but then she does have a very special mindset."

"A special mindset?" Captain Garcia smiled, intrigued. "How interesting. What exactly do you mean?"

"She's religious, you know, Roman Catholic background. We made the mistake of placing her with the nuns as a little girl, Salesians down in Marbella, a wonderful teaching order. Yes, she suddenly wanted to be a nun. A rather intense child."

"Yes," said Jose, "my sister, little sister also wanted to 'marry Christ', I think they call it. My mother used to make comments and the girl would not like it. A bit of a brainwash, I think, but a few months later it wore off. Just another fad."

"Well, being a very intense child, Sally Anne wanted to understand it further and developed an interest in the writings of a saint, a nun named Teresa of Jesus, of Avila."

"Who are these people, Roberto?" demanded a strident woman's voice. The three men stood up and Jose spoke.

"We are from the police, madame. Just conducting some routine enquiries in the area."

"I see," she retorted grandly. "I did hear you mention my daughter as I entered just now. Surely Sally Anne has not been getting into any scrapes. It's not in her nature."

"No," said Jose; "of course not, just that in the course of our conversation we somehow digressed into the field of

Roman Catholic saints. Your husband mentioned your daughter's interest in Saint Teresa of Avila, I believe?"

"Yes, of course. I'm Wendy Diez, by the way, or Cotton if we follow the local system. Yes, Saint Teresa was known as a mystic saint. A fascinating woman."

"Yes," joined in Roberto, warming to the subject. "The girl did become something of a mystic herself, reading up Sufism and searching for Shahada. She spent some time in a school in Marrakech. Also took an interest in the Moksha of the Hindus, hahaha, but we drew the line when she decided to go to India."

"And the Nizari Ismailis, I suppose?" asked Jose.

"Not really," retorted Robert. "Yes, they were mystics, but they were the assassin sect." And then, realising what he had just said, he looked at both of the officers blankly.

"Well, we must be getting on now," said Juan. "Thank you both so much."

"Won't you have some tea?" Mrs Diez asked. "You can't leave without a cup of tea."

"We are so grateful, Mrs Diez, but duty calls. By the way, perhaps you'd be so kind as to ask Sally Anne and her two friends Colia and Peter to please phone police headquarters and make an appointment to see me. Just ask for Juan Betardo."

Once the policemen had driven off, Mrs Diez called for her daughter. She and her husband walked out to the lounge area behind the house, where they found Sally Anne and her two friends.

"That was the police. They want to see all you children."
"Whatever for?" asked Peter and Sally Anne.

"Dis is just like Rashia, just like Rashiaa."

"Shut up, Colia. Sorry, he gets stupid sometimes," said Peter. "I think you are suspects in the shooting of the Senator." Colia burst out laughing. "We are de ones. We are gilti." "That's a Ghana accent, you dope."

Sally Anne had gone all quiet. "It's Alarico they're after, you know. But he's gone, he's gone to Gaza."

"Good grief," retorted her mother. "Whatever for? There's nothing in Gaza – just terrorists."

"There are children mother, suffering children. Eighty percent of the children in Gaza are clinically depressed. They've committed no crime, just living there and being Palestinian. Alarico couldn't live with himself anymore and do nothing. He said to me that as a doctor he should be where he is needed, mother, and that's not the Costa del Sol."

"Why did you do that, Jose? They are nice people and you just drew them into your little trap. They are not killers, my friend, neither they nor their children. They are just normal decent people."

"Juan, we are police officers. You are really developing a fondness for our prime suspect, and now for his people. I agree he does seem a nice person, but he is most likely a killer. Dostoyevsky's characters were in many cases nice, even religious, and yet capable of suicide, and fratricide. Look at Kirov, the engineer who killed himself over the idea that it was his right to do so. It doesn't make it right. It's wrong to take a life."

"I know," said Juan. "You're right, of course. It's just that all the time in the back of my head is the thought that what is motivating our killer is the wanton murder that major states are perpetrating, ostensibly in the name of politics, but really for personal gain.

"In any event, I have ordered my secretary to obtain court orders for the search of the O'Donovan finca and all the surrounding area for two kilometres in any direction."

"Why in heaven's name, Jose?"

"Because I am following your argument. This was not any killer, this was an enlightened person that killed this Senator. By the way, my secretary told me that a second press release has appeared in which our killer claims the second killing, the Ruben Misrahi assassination. She's sending us both copies on our cells. Also, I am trying to keep Madrid off our backs, as I am sure Laura will have informed, in a lame manner of course, that we are on a walkabout while she is holding the fort.

"I just get the strangest feeling based on our various conversations that there's more than meets the eye here. The talk about mysticism and subsequently the assassins. And didn't you notice that everyone we've spoken to describes the suspect as crazy and erratic, but also as strange? Now what exactly is strange about him? That's what I would like to know."

"You were the one who mentioned the assassins. Just about stymied the poor fellow. He was just conversing."

"No, Juan, think. It was him. I just mentioned the Nizari Ismaelis, and he then uttered the word assassins, and then realised what he had said."

"But you led them and embarrassed them. They both had the grace to be embarrassed. She had the class to try to gloss it over with tea."

"Yes, the British do have that, their tea, their tea wins wars, but, Saint Teresa, Sufis, the Ismaili are a natural progression. If you look back through Ismaeli history, followers of the young Imam Hadi who wished to be fighters were trained as Fidai (Fedayeen), whose bravery and self-sacrificing spirituality came from their belief that the Nizari *Imam-ul-Waqt* ("Imam of the time") had the Noor (light) of God within him. These became our assassins, and our killer also claims to be God's instrument."

"Yes." conceded Juan. "I suppose there is a parallel between the killer's declaration and the Fidai. But still, Jose, I don't like this one little bit. It's radical overplay, reminiscent of Franco's times. At what time do the troops move in?"

"Well, the judge has given the go-ahead. The uniformed Guardia and police commanders are doing the planning, and I have given and signed your and my authorities. We move in at two pm."

"I wish you wouldn't do that, Jose."

At exactly two pm the Guardia Civil closed all access roads to anywhere in the Entrerrios area or within a two-kilometre limit. Seprona, the division of the Guardia dedicated to patrolling the countryside on mountain bikes, closed off all pathways and set up a physical perimeter to prevent all access or egress from the area.

People having their lunch at Elias's *Venta* were amazed when Guardia Civil and National Police riot vans and troop carriers began to arrive. Mr O'Donovan was just returning from a horse ride and was requested to return to his house and remain there at the disposal of the police. This he did after much hearty protestation, as a preferred alternative to arrest.

ANSAKI DEVOUT

Chapter Fifteen:
Doctors of Love

Gaza

In a darkened alleyway somewhere in the greater Ismailia area close to Fumm-el-Khaliq in El Cairo is the office or delegation of "Doctors of Love". The flat is on the fourth, top floor, where the sun does shine, and a delightfully green garden is kept on the large terrace, oblivious to the protests of the downstairs neighbours who suffer from damp.

A large, overweight man was sitting ensconced in a generous cane armchair right at the back of the gazebo. He was dressed in a white suit and surrounded by plants, some small and others overhanging. It was not hot due to the various fans, big powerful noisy machines, some blowing their indiscreet but welcoming blasts at him, others in random directions.

"Many think we are a dating setup, hahaha," he laughed, wiping his perspiring brow with a large handkerchief. Perhaps we are, all these young romantic doctors. But no, sir, we are committed to bringing love to the truly in need, although I can assure you that there is more love in tiny Gaza than in many of those enormous American cities, where it seems to many of us that they have totally lost the plot.

"But these, our aid recipients, are so physically and mentally exhausted from many years of being at the mercy of a power that would gladly exterminate them, that they need love from the hands of professionals adept in those arts that will truly help and soothe them, and especially the majority of the population there who are children. As you will imagine we have well-qualified applicants applying to us from all around the globe, hoping to be given a chance to practice their profession in our Holy Land, so we do need to know the ins and outs of a cat's behind concerning who they are and why they want to help."

"Well Sir, Effendi," replied a young, tall, fresh-faced fellow seated before him in a straight- backed cane chair, together with two other men. Both were white-skinned, one a Spaniard of Catalan descent, the other an Egyptian. "I am a nobody who lives on a Spanish coast and wastes his life. I hear about these children, and am desperate to do something worthwhile."

"You mean like, "and to die for a cause?" The fat man intoned the single stanza of the popular Garfunkel song with a knowledgeable air and a desultory chuckle, suggesting a faint irritation at the young man's excessive humility.

"Carthy," stated the youth with apparent enthusiasm. "Probably," agreed the Catalan. "I think it was."

The fat man looked on perplexed. Then he suddenly banged the table with his large and hairy right hand. "I don't give a gnat's fart what either of you think, it was Garfunkel."

The Catalan man looked rather shocked and taken aback by the large man's insistent assertion of his opinion on the subject, having assumed that the item was open to friendly discussion. He was, of course, labouring under the misapprehension that like in Spain, people would discuss everything, often all speaking at the same time.

"A tinker's cuss, a damn, even a fuck, but a gnat's fart?" said the tall young man and giggled hilariously.

"Are you a doctor sir, a medical doctor?" demanded the large man in a loud tone.

"I am indeed Sahib. I am a family doctor," he said with an exaggerated Pakistani accent. "Here are my credentials," he said, slipping some clipped documents out of a case. "And by the way, how about some tea?"

"I am not a Sahib, I am neither Indian nor Pakistani, I am a Jew and naturalised Egyptian by nationality. I was originally Swedish, although my family was once Spanish. But let me see, it's you we are discussing here. I am told you want to go to Gaza to help the children. And here, I don't need your papers. I already have them, and indeed the Egyptian Ministry of Health, represented by my friend Doctor Omar Mohamed el Abasi, knows all about you."

The Egyptian doctor nodded amiably toward them. He was seated on a cane chair, a cross between the straight-backed ones the two Spaniards were seated on and the throne the host was using. He had sat through the interchange quietly amused and mystified as to what had set it off, as the fat man had told him confidentially that the young man would most definitely be going to Gaza.

The tall young man stood up and put his hands together and bowed toward the Egyptian. "Greetings from Europe, Bab. La, do you understand a leetle of our talking please, Bab La?"

The Egyptian man smiled, and the fat man spoke for him.

"Please Doctor O'Donovan, Doctor Omar does speak English you know, just the smattering he picked up at Oxford and later at Yale. His Spanish I understand is also impeccable, so I think we may dispense with the sign language and the pigeon English."

The Egyptian official lifted a cautious hand to indicate that he would speak.

"Entering Gaza, Doctor," looking also towards the second Spaniard, "is hardly the most pleasant of trips. We have decided, and I think Moshe agrees," he said, nodding toward the fat man, "that our best shot at getting you in is to include you with the delegation of Egyptian doctors due to go over in just two days. This visit has been agreed upon between ministers, so they should, hopefully, not give us excess trouble. Your papers have already been submitted to the Israeli authorities, and the story is that you are a special consultant dealing with stress- related ailments and manifestations in children."

"What do you mean, the story is?" retorted O'Donovan. "What on earth have you been told? Just because he is wrong about Carthy doesn't mean…"

His Catalan friend nudged him discreetly with the tip of his shoe. "Ouch! What was that for?"

"Alarico, for heaven's sake, they are the ones arranging your visit to Gaza, but at some juncture, if you continue with your inane behavior, we will be thrown out."

The Egyptian, fearing any further heated and nonsensical exchanges, again put out his hand as if requesting permission to speak further.

"Perhaps you would like to ask your wonderful daughter Esther if she would like to accompany these gentlemen to the teashop at the end of the alley for some refreshment while we sort out the details of the visit," suggested the Egyptian.

"Yes indeed," beamed Moshe, whose demeanour changed completely once the name Esther was mentioned. "That is a good idea." He unceremoniously grabbed a liana that hung from the roof and pulled it vigorously.

They all stood up as a young woman of perhaps twenty-six or seven entered the gazebo, having been summoned by the maid who had answered the bell. She shook hands first with the Egyptian official, whom she knew, and then with Geordi the Catalan, and finally with Alarico.

"So you're going into the Strip," she enquired pleasantly. "That's quite brave of you," she said, looking freshly and silently up into his face.

"Well, we will be once we get over this Scarborough Fair nonsense." He grimaced. The girl just smiled.

"They have wonderful chai with nana and freshly baked halva," she said. "As soon as you're ready we can go."

"I'm ready, we're ready," he chirped up instantly. Leaning over, he whispered, "It's just him," into her ear, indicating her father with his eyes. "Argumentative sort." And then, "Come on, Geordi, the nana and halva await, and *konyeshno*" (Russian for "of course") "the company of the mysterious Esther." He swept out of the door with the two in tow, looking at each other with resigned glances, Geordie gallantly ushering the girl before them as they went.

"I suppose you dance, Esther?" enquired the tall youth with a backward glance. "Yes, of course. Barefoot sometimes. I dance all the Palestinian dances."

"Wonderful, wonderful, wonderful. You will teach me now please, it will be an important part of my therapy for the little ones." He waltzed back to where she was just descending the last stair and, grasping her in an embrace, waltzed around with her. She laughed good-naturedly and followed his lead, although with a certain stiffness and reserve, a demure reticence, which added to her overall charm. She must have measured some one sixty metres, perhaps sixty- five. There was a determination about her, softened by her gentleness and the beauty of her face, and indeed her shape and general demeanour.

She spun out of his embrace, dancing and looking back smiling as she went.

"Come," she commanded jestingly, as if the tall, wonderfully handsome stranger she had just met was a child. "Come, you will learn the dance of all dances, a song straight from the Levant from Palestine: the Dabke."

"Are you from Palestine?" "From Jerusalem."

"But your father, he is your father? Is a Jew?"

"He is a good man, he loves and serves God. His religion and race don't matter. But yes, he is a Jew and proud to be one, and so am I, a Palestinian Jew. I am also a Muslim, as was my mother. You see, for us, a creed as such is only a road. One can follow many roads. If the roads clash you can be sure that there are evil men behind it trying to create dissent for power or money."

Alarico followed her silently.

"I am Geordie, and this is Alarico. We are both doctors. I work in Spain as a coordinator and fundraiser for Doctors of Love, and this is my first visit to Egypt."

Set back from the road as they emerged from the alley, an old house served as a café to a small group of patrons accommodated at wooden tables on an outside terrace.

"An old Mamluk house, they say," she began but was interrupted as Alarico suddenly sprang out of the shade of the alley and into the café. Through the large windows, they could see a small stage inside the building, on to which Alarico leapt and began to bang his heels and feet on the wooden surface. An old man sitting by the stage wearing a tarboosh grinned at Esther as she entered, and began to play an old oud that lay at his side, marking time with Alarico's stamping. Esther kicked off her shoes and jumped onto the platform. "Sevillanas," she shouted to the strummer, and Alarico changed his movement and together they performed the first two routines of the dance from Seville.

"Geordie, come join us," she panted. "Now we dance the Dabke."

She leapt off the stage, dragged him up, and beckoned two of the old men who were standing around clapping to the rhythm. They formed in a line, and she and the old men led jumping, skipping, leg waving, whilst Alarico and Geordie tied themselves into a knot trying to follow the movements and the drum that had suddenly appeared and was sounding away vigorously.

"How long have we been at it?" gasped a collapsed Geordie to one of the newcomers to the dance. "Five minutes," laughed the man. "Very vigorous, takes time, the old men have been doing it since they were kids of four and five."

Later they all sat around a table laden with sweetmeats and halva, the girl, the Spaniard, Moshe, and Omar, who had probably tired of waiting and come down knowing that it would all have culminated with a Dabke. They drank strong Egyptian tea brewed with nana, mint, and sweetly sugared.

"God it's sweet."

"That's how we drink it, Geordie. The Egyptian heat soon dissipates the effect of the sugar."

"How soon will he be polished enough to teach the Dabke? Look at him." Alarico was still dancing on the stage, the sweat visibly dripping off him, with a bunch of men who were laughing and correcting him as he led the line.

"He won't need to – the children will teach him. For years I taught them to dance." "Will you cross with him then?"

"No, no more Gaza for me. I am forbidden," she said vehemently as she glanced up at her father, who was listening in on the conversation. Then she stood up and swept from the room, disappearing into the darkening street. Geordie made to follow her, but Moshe leaned over the table and placed a restraining hand on his forearm.

"Please let her go. You will be so kind, just remain here and enjoy the delights they have served up." Then he changed seats and came to join Geordie. "Who is he?" he beckoned with his chin. "Who is that Alarico, who is he under the act?"

"I think you have an idea, Moshe, perhaps a better idea than I," said the Spaniard.

"I always wish and I often dream that someone really special comes along and does something truly momentous. We send doctors in now and again but the challenge is so great. But this time I am full of expectations. I realise you would not suspect it from our childish interchange before, but sometimes it takes a little pointless sparring to see who a person is. Quite frankly, however, I am at as much of a loss as before, except for one highly relevant factor that you would decry as superstitious, but about which I will not at present speak further. I can only say that I was awaiting this individual with bated breath."

"Well said, Geordie. Nobody knows him completely, he's very deep and good and angelic and scary, and so gentle, and yet I am sure he can be utterly lethal. Oh, and he's an absolute nutcase. Having said all of that, I have absolutely no idea of what his intentions are, other than what he says."

"And what is it that he says?" "Ask him," said Geordie.

"You do work for us, you know."

"If I thought you meant what you just said I would stand up, tell you to F. off, and walk away. But I don't think so. I know lots about people. You could be a spy for the Zionists, you are a Jew, after all. You could be many things. Why don't you tell me, who is Moshe and who is Esther? That would certainly be a start. Oh! And while you're at it, you may as well tell me what it was that you saw in Alarico that inspired you."

"I apologise, Geordie. I appreciate your loyalty to the man."

"Hardly loyalty," barked Geordie. "I only met him a week ago. What I know of him is either assimilated in the last few days or what I have been told. Personal experience tells me that the guy is a total lunatic, completely inane yet charming and that he does want to help. But it doesn't all add up. Now your turn. Tell me why we should trust you."

The fat man glanced around the room to where Omar sat at a table in a far corner talking animatedly with a beautiful young Egyptian girl.

"He's intelligence, Egyptian, directly through to the dictator Sisi, I believe. Liaises with all the orgs operating in and out of Gaza and the West Bank. Ostensibly he's a high-up in the Medical Ministry with a line through to the minister himself.

"I have been in trade here in El Cairo for many years, and married a Palestinian girl. She was a nurse, very dedicated, and an incredibly wonderful woman. I became the local delegate for Doctors of Love on her insistence; it was my way of holding hands with her over Gaza, which was to all intents and purposes her life work. On the sixteenth of May of 2021, the Israelis bombed Gaza. They bombed the hospital close to the clinic of Médecins sans Frontières. She died, along with ten children."

His large head bowed and he was silent, a silence that for Geordie at that moment was louder than the most vibrant music. "I curse Likud, I curse the Zionists, I curse Israelis for their compliance and support for these criminals, and I curse every Jew everywhere who is not raising his or her voice in protest against these devils.

"D'you know," he shouted, "they bomb all the essential infrastructure, water, electricity, sewage. They even bombed the access roads to the hospitals so that the many injured cannot get help. And what do I do as my restitution for the evil being perpetrated by my own brothers in religion? I send doctors to help to fight the mental traumas dominating the child victims. If I were true I would go to Tel Aviv and truly do something about it, something, not just sit here. You have come from Spain. There a man killed a Senator and claimed justification for doing so. I have read his press release, which was available through many social media, cleverly disguised, and yet it went completely viral. I helped in my tiny way by sending it on to the limit of my ability, although it resulted in my being blocked from various social websites for weeks."

"Perhaps you should be more discreet in your opinions," replied Geordie with a gentle smile. The older man took his forearm in the grasp of one of his gorilla-like paws and looking into the Catalan's face whispered hoarsely, "Perhaps they think I am a pathetic widower carrying a candle for his lost love. They see my rantings as part of my inanity. I am harmless, I am useful. In fact, my friend, I think I recently came across an approximate image of myself, a Spaniard. Perhaps one day I will be an angel, a saint, and what may come?"

"But you have not told me why this lunatic is special," Geordi asked, "why you have, as you termed it, a superstitious expectation."

But the large man had, contrary to all of Geordi's appraisals of him, suddenly leapt up from the table and danced his way across the floor to join the line doing the Dabke, despite his substantial bulk. The other men greeted him raucously, and the young Catalan realised that there was more to this man than met the eye.

ANSAKI DEVOUT

Chapter Sixteen:
Via Rafah to Gaza

"He's snoring," smiled Fatima, one of the younger nurses, in a whisper.

"He's been at it since we left Cairo since you stopped chattering to him," snorted Ana, an older colleague, "and where he thinks he's going in those yellow trousers and that ridiculous hair I can't imagine."

The medical convoy was equipped mainly with European money and equipment and staffed entirely by Egyptians, all destined for Gaza and its beleaguered people. It swept along the main Cairo to Gaza highway, on its way to its first obstacle, the Suez Canal, a crossing by ferry, and then onwards to the small border town of El Arish and the infamous Rafah crossing.

There were four doctors and six nurses travelling in a Mercedes minibus in a convoy of four vehicles emblazoned with Red Crescent emblems on all sides and the roofs of the vehicles. The other vehicles consisted of two very new-looking, fully equipped portable clinics and a van for medical supplies and equipment.

"He's a doctor," smiled Fatima, "a special doctor for children, it says on the documents, an expert on stress-related problems. Maybe he's dressed specially."

"I think he's an idiot," said Ana. "He kissed me on the top of my head when we were introduced."

"Well, he kissed my hand and wouldn't let it go, bowing over it and saying Guapa, Guapa, till Doctor El Zandawi started clearing his throat loudly and he got the hint, but he's not like that at all, he's just sort of special."

"And what did you go on about so long, talking and talking in Spanish so we couldn't understand?"

"The younger girl blushed. He's just interested in everything, about the Strip and here and about the crossing and the kids and... Well, it's a rare chance for me to practice my Spanish."

"And then he just goes and falls asleep on you."

The younger girl just leaned back in her seat. She let her thoughts run away with her. A strange combination of impressions had come over her. He was so good-looking and yet childlike, and very gentlemanly, and then the Spanish side of him, another contrast.

"Come sit here at the back," he had said, and Dr El Zandawi and a couple of the other doctors had raised their glances, but not said anything.

So she went. He asked her why people said the crossing was so bad.

"So bad!" she had exclaimed in an angry tone, caught unawares. "Three hundred and eighteen kilometres, we'll do it in a few hours, the Palestinians sometimes take as long as four days. The Egyptian army treats them like shit, like vermin."

"I'm so sorry," he said. He leaned over and touched her arm. She smiled.

"No, I'm sorry," she answered apologetic and friendly again. "You see, I'm Palestinian. You weren't to know it. I married an Egyptian. I met him working as a nurse. I once travelled both ways with my *hawiyya*, my Palestinian ID card. It was hell." She lowered her voice to a whisper. One of the medics travelling with them glanced over.

"They set out to dehumanise us in every way. The checkpoint before the Ferdan ferry, the Suez Canal crossing is the first in a string of tortures. They check every item of luggage, and there are no benches like anywhere normal, they scatter your stuff on the sandy floor and kick it around if you happen to get a soldier who's in a bad mood, I had to wait ten hours. There are no toilets, no food, no water, and no shelter. Then they confiscate whatever takes their fancy, electronic goods, wrapped presents, computers, and cameras. When you get through and cross the Suez on the ferry thinking it's all over you relax. Then you realise it's only just begun. There are fifteen more checkpoints before you arrive at El Arish and the Rafah crossing.

"At every checkpoint, we were made to wait in the blazing sun. It was summer, so you can imagine. Now it's September. If we tried conversing with people from other cars the soldiers would threaten us with their guns. We needed to find spots away from the enormous waiting crowds to perform our ablutions, you know, to go to the toilet. We had to sleep wherever we could although many travelling in overcrowded cars slept on the roadside. There were old people, often incapacitated, and babies who cried throughout.

"The final customs hall into which we all piled to show our documents was in the filthiest state imaginable, with no rubbish bins, shit on the floor, rubbish everywhere. We were crowded in, and the onlooking soldiers would look at us with disgust as if we were animals. Again they kept us waiting for hours while they played with their phones, and then let us through with only the most cursory of glances at our documents.

"Of course, for seven hundred to five thousand dollars per person, you can travel in luxury. There is a company named Da Mala that operates these tours, it seems that they are owned by the Egyptian military. So that the reason to make these people suffer so much for several days, is to encourage them to pay for VIP treatment for the benefit of some general. And this is all before we even come up against the Israelis."

The convoy came slowly to a stop.

"Egyptian army people waving us down," shouted the driver.

An imperious knocking sounded on the window. The driver opened and the hot September air poured into the van, heralding the arrival of a uniformed person. He stepped in and saluted slightly.

"Dr Zandawi, I am Captain Alami of the Egyptian Ground Forces. Orders from Cairo. We are redirecting you for your comfort across the canal bridge at Quantara. I will lead you there; please instruct your drivers to follow my jeep."

"Excuse me, excuse me," They all looked up at the voice coming from the rear of the van.

The Spanish doctor who was now in a sitting position pointed at the bemused Egyptian captain.

"Alexandria," he said loudly. Silence reigned. The doctors were all aghast. Here they were in an army-dominated area and one of their doctors was accosting an officer. The officer continued to look in the direction of the Spaniard as if waiting for more.

"I am so sorry," spluttered Zandawi, only to be waved down in a friendly fashion by the captain, who glanced at him, and then turned his attention back to the Spaniard with the ghost of a smile on his face.

"Al Ittihad, Al Ittihad," the Spaniard chanted, waving his fists in the air. Two thousand nine, I was there. We drew." He pointed at the Egyptian officer's chest and then back at his own where a small yellow badge nestled. "Real Madrid, champions of the world."

The officer suddenly burst out laughing. "Al Ittihad, Al Ittihad," he said, pointing to his own badge, green with a tiger's head. "Champions of Africa and Asia. I also was there. I went with my father. We thought we would lose but we drew, and many Spaniards told us we deserved to win three-nil. Come ride with me in my jeep. You can return to the van after we cross the bridge. With your permission, Dr. El Zandawi, I will practise a little of my terrible Spanish."

The cavalcade set off anew, following its military escort and Alarico O'Donovan de Medinacheli, who rejoined them after a drive of some forty minutes, full of the joys of spring and sporting a football scarf that his newfound friend happened to be carrying in his jeep.

"It is written that we should meet today, my friend. I just collected this scarf this morning, and now you. I don't know if you believe in fate, but I do," he said, and despite Alarico's strongest protests and refusals, the scarf was foisted upon him until he finally and gratefully accepted it.

Alarico sat together with the other doctors and on the aisle opposite Fatima. Dr Zandawi looked up from his paper and over the rim of his spectacles. "I trust you enjoyed your trip with your new friend?"

"Wonderful, the bridge was amazing. Some of those tall masts on the shipping seem barely able to scrape through. Got enough names, the bridge."

"Yes, and one more he probably didn't tell you about Tcharou, for the historic city situated on the ancient Egyptian military road, the Way of Horus, into Canaan, also known as Sele."

"He mentioned that it was also known as the Mubarak Peace Bridge and that it was mainly financed by the Japanese. And then we spoke of other things."

"Football, I suppose," said Zandawi.

"Naw, we don't like football it transpired, neither of us. He follows it for his dad and now for his son and I, well, I just am erratic about what attracts my attention at any given time. Well, to pass the time I asked him why the Egyptian military treat the Palestinians like shit."

"You never did!" exclaimed Fatima with her hand at her mouth.

"Well, I phrased it differently. He just ignored me, so I insisted. Then he said, for the benefit of his driver, I imagine, 'Leave it alone or I'll throw you in the canal.'"

"You and who's army," I shouted back, and suddenly realised what I'd said and where I was, and we both burst out laughing. I said, but don't you care? And he replied, there's little I can do about it. I said that's what the SS German soldiers said at Nuremberg. He said, speak to the surviving Jewish Holocaust victims about what is happening in Palestine. They are very angry and protest constantly, but can do nothing."

Anna and Fatima sat looking at him, open-mouthed.

"He does have a point," said one of the young doctors. "There's so much evil around these days that one just feels helpless against it." A total silence descended until Alarico changed the subject.

"I used to think that Sinai was a beautiful place full of rich olive groves and fertile lands, whitewashed farmhouses, and prosperous towns. It figures as a tourist destination on the internet."

"Part of it may still be as before, after all, it's big enough," replied a recovered Fatima. "All I know is that since 2013 this area has been a battleground between militants and the military, and the Egyptian army has done an Attila on it. Completely wiped it out."

The countryside they motored through was invariably grey or brown, not a tree, not a house. Everything, towns, and villages were all razed by the military to stop them from serving as havens for the Bedouins who were the main militants.

In 2013, a military coup in Egypt had ousted the legitimately elected Islamic government of Mohamed El Morsi, an intellectual who died in 2019 in prison under mysterious circumstances. Thousands of members of the Arab Brotherhood, Morsi's party, were killed, tortured, and imprisoned by the military. and the opposition by militants began and continues today.

Fatima watched silently as his eyes began to close. He seemed to have a talent for slipping off to sleep, but then he had been travelling and probably had a backlog to catch up on. They sat there, she and Ana, as the depressing kilometres of destroyed countryside slipped by. After a while, he began to snore.

"You know where he's from?" asked a young doctor, turning around in his seat and answering without awaiting a reply. "He's from Spain, from Malaga. You know it's in the papers, the manhunt for the Robin Hood Killer."

"Could be him," put in another young doctor. "Doesn't look the part though. Anna looks more of a killer than him." They both laughed.

Another voice, clearing his throat, and they looked up to see Alarico, awake and swinging his dreadlocks off his face with a sharp tossing movement.

"There's a part of me I am not familiar with. As with all of us, we don't know how we would react to an immediate threat against those we love, or to our physical integrity. And when I saw so many videos and photographs depicting the hapless plight of the Palestinian people, I came, in the hope that when the bombs began to fall or I was fired on by soldiers, or when the children were in need, that I would not flinch or run, and dare to stand before oppression. And as to whether or not I am the killer from Spain, it's a matter of conjecture for me as much as for the rest of you, because if I am it is yet another of those parts of me of which I am not aware."

"Touché, Sir, most succinctly put." Dr El Zandawi looked up over his spectacles. "If you are discreetly frowning upon our frivolity in this air-conditioned bus, which was supplied by the colonisers, of today or yesterday, whilst Palestinian travellers suffer humiliation and mistreatment over days to make the same journey, I can only say that we at least make the journey to aid and assist these people."

"Well, if you are the Spanish Ansaki, I've read your press release and can't say I disagree with much of what you say," said the first of the younger doctors.

"It is murder, though, you know," said the other," although it's true that we are seeing so much illegal killing everywhere these days that it makes one wonder."

"Which means," burst out the first, "that you've also read the confession written by the phantom assassin, the incitement to all the young and illuminated all over the world to kill off their favourite local corrupt politician or similar bad hat, whatever you wish to term it."

"Perhaps it would be wiser to forget the subject altogether, given that it's hardly likely that Doctor O'Donovan is this person just because he comes from the same area in Spain."

Chapter Seventeen:
Gaza

"When I was with the children it was as if I was transported into a different world. When I appeared, wondering how to begin, they were very nice and well-behaved and dignified, and yet I considered that we would have time for being serious later, so I started cavorting around, something I was good at, and then I put some Spanish music on the speaker of my mobile and I danced.

"They looked at me wide-eyed, then one little boy laughed and imitated me and so I danced with them all one at a time. All of them, even the quietest and most unwilling, finally gave way under the onslaught of my barrage of unassailable stupidities, my repertoire of items, of inanities, collected over the years to irritate people back home.

"Stupid things like exaggerated nose-picking from different angles involving my whole body and, in a similar OTT fashion, arse-scratching, laughing, sneezing, yawning. All the while I was asking myself by what right I was there at all in this state of mind and intruding on their bravery.

"Children were so eager to laugh and be entertained, especially this little lot. They had so much to put behind them, and the worst part was that they were scared by the fact that the warplanes could be back at any time to continue their horrendous war against children here in

Gaza. But it was only later that I became aware of this, as they worked so hard at being cheerful that they had even me conned.

"Then, when we were not dancing and playing, they would come often with their parents, if they still had any, or with their brothers or sisters or a friend, and I would listen. Every day they came, they came when they could and it was late into the night, so my only free time was to eat and sleep, but I wanted to hear them, to hear every word that they needed to get off their little chests.

"Every child had problems. Some didn't sleep at night and you could see it etched on their little exhausted faces. Others would cry and tell me about their brothers and sisters who were caught in the bombings, and they would tell me that they had felt no pain and gone straight to Allah. But some would cry and say that they were still alive somewhere. There were those little ones who wet their beds at night, and others who ate very badly and often needed to be fed intravenously. One little boy had stopped speaking altogether when the bombs began to drop. The list was endless; they were all disturbed in one way or another.

"And then there were those many who had lost limbs or had been hit by shrapnel from bombs or debris. Two little girls had lost both limbs. There were thank God various centres run by people, wonderful people from different countries, who worked hard with these children. My Lord in heaven, who are these devils who are committing these acts against a population that they have trapped within a narrow strip of land, only to bomb them at their whim, targeting residential buildings and little children?

"One day the sirens went off in another place by mistake, and some of the children were hysterical, screaming crying clutching each other, and running around in terror. I immediately switched my phone to El Daalaona dance music and began to dance the Dabke. Two boys who had told me that they would be fighters immediately they were permitted joined in, and we formed the line which grew as the children calmed down. I did all my usual antics and did my best to get them to laugh and shout, even though I was shit scared. I wasn't hero material.

"Throughout all of this, there were always some young guys hanging around watching. I felt that they were not judging me, just hoping that I would be special and would bring something magical tucked under my arm. They took me around to the different places where I would see the children."

One day they took him around Gaza to see the devastation caused by the aerial attacks. He didn't seem interested in the political reasoning at all, they later told investigators from the UN but was angered to learn that the majority of the targets were civilian infrastructure, including eighteen hospitals or clinics or medical centres, electricity generating plants, water storage facilities, and fuel depots. The fishermen who were constantly harassed by gunboats and occasionally sunk when the gunboats opened fire, again as a whim, were one of the food sources of the embattled Strip. They spoke to him and explained their plight. He was amazed and could hardly believe it when they told him of the four boys playing football on the beach being shot to death by a gunboat as potential terrorists. Four kids kicking a football. It appeared on the news in those few places in the world allowed to learn of the atrocity. Nothing was done, at all. Four little boys were dead, shot down in cold blood by a handful of Israel's psychopathic occupation force, for the crime of playing football.

The boys took him to meet an old lady who had lost all her family. She made him sit down and made all the boys sit down. They laughed and joked with her. Two of them were fighters (resistance), and the other three were just lads who had come along, and she gave them all soup. As they left, he gave her money, which she refused. Then she kissed him and thanked him with great dignity, and they went.

He hadn't slept since he got to Gaza, for days. There was a bed for him at one of the places they had set up as hospitals. As they walked through the dark, bomb-cratered streets, it dawned on him in a flash that they could be walking at night in the streets of his own town in Spain, a place named Fuengirola, where people, young people could walk freely through peaceful streets and shout and be drunk and laugh and not be murdered by a rain of random bombs. He walked silently, they looked at him, and they saw, the tears pouring down his face, hidden by his long, thick, dreadlocked hair, and some of the boys linked arms with him and they patted him. They left him there, sitting on his bed in the darkness, with just the faint moonlight filtering in.

He thought he must have seemed ridiculous to those tough kids crying like that. He took a razor from his pack and began to shave his long dreadlocks off. He ran his hand over his shaven head. There were lumps and irritations he did not know were there. When they came to find him in the morning, he washed as well as he could with the bucket of cold water that was supplied, as water was scarce.

This day the children in the school he visited were older and told him of what was happening in the West Bank and how children were being grabbed by soldiers at night while they slept in the warmth and privacy of their beds, or in the daytime on their way to school, freshly scrubbed and bright as new pennies, and beaten and arrested with no charge or accusation. They told him that children were afraid to go out of their homes for fear of arrest, fearfully and tearfully gazing out of the street windows, delaying the moment for as long as they could. Many of the children would be locked up on their own in a dirty cell for two weeks or a month and then questioned and beaten and told what to say when they went to court and made to sign confessions in Israeli, a language they did not understand at all.

They told him about the settlers who wanted the Palestinians to leave, so they would stone the children and sometimes attack them, and once they threw acid at a girl.

They were always accompanied by soldiers who protected them in case any Palestinian adult tried to defend the children, in which case the soldiers would carry the man, woman, or child off, often wounded and bleeding. But the Palestinian people had nowhere to go, this was their home. The army would throw the families out and bulldoze their homes, thousands of them, and the soldiers would attack the cities and kill the people if they dared to protest.

When the young children who knew him saw him, they laughed and pulled him down so they could touch his shaved head.

And then he was gone. Many children asked for him all the time, but nobody knew where he was. Then they learned that he was in West Bank, in Jerusalem. How he got there is a mystery, as only Palestinian workers can cross at the Erez crossing.

Chapter Eighteen:
Tel Aviv

It was late evening when Chief Inspector Juan Betardo of the Spanish National Police strode absentmindedly across the expanse of tarmac that separated the entrance of the air terminal at Ben Gurion Airport from the Spanish Air Iberia flight he had just flown in on. It was his first time visiting Israel. He was accompanied by a very large man, his friend Pyotr Lebedev, a Russian national travelling with him at his request and that of the Spanish police and government.

"They make me nervous, all these Israelis rushing around. They remind me of when I watched the news the day they assassinated Yitzhak Rabin. It was like watching people from outer space dashing around and wailing. Some say that Netanyahu, the present president, had a hand in it directly or indirectly."

"I'd watch my mouth if I were you," said his gruff companion as he glanced around at their fellow passengers who were walking with them across the still-hot airport tarmac flooded by lights streaming from the overhead lamps and the main building. "This isn't Spain. To all intents and purposes, we are in a police state, so if you prefer to stay free of hassle then we should not discuss, Israel, Palestine, or the Arabs."

"Fuck them," retorted Betardo. "They're hardly likely to arrest me. Anyway, the normal man in the street has little to do with what's going on."

"I was thinking more in terms of you accidentally getting shot when we get to the West Bank. Some interchange of fire between terrorists and the IOF troops and, what a disaster, Spanish policeman killed outright, nobody knows for sure where the bullet came from, the same as happened to that US reporter. And let me put you right. Since Rabin was murdered – when was it, in 95? – and Likud and their cronies got in, there's been a massive 're-education' of the populus, the man in the street as you term it, in particular, the youth. There they come now," he whistled through his teeth. "Probably heard you on their famous spy gear – directional mikes."

A white police jeep, its blue lights flashing, drove slowly across the tarmac toward the advancing passengers. Two uniformed men and another casually dressed in jeans and a pullover wearing a kippah got out and walked toward them.

"Chief Inspector Juan Betardo?"

"That's right. Good evening, very good I must say. We haven't even made it to the terminal building and have already alerted the local constabulary. How did you recognise me in the relative darkness and at such a distance?"

"Not you, Chief Inspector, the man with you is known to us. Welcome to Israel, Mr Lebedev, Pyotr."

"Thank you," retorted Lebedev curtly. "And who exactly is welcoming me?"

"Well, Sir," said the man in civilian attire, "this is Agent Aaron Peres from, well he works with the Jerusalem NCB office, that is Europol and Interpol. He will be working with you and will accompany you in your visit to West Bank. He is INP of course. And this," indicating the second uniformed man, "is Chief Inspector Moses Hassan, Judicial Brigade for all four districts, also Israeli National police, your counterpart here in Israel, Chief Inspector Betardo."

Betardo stepped forward smilingly and shook hands with all three men. Lebedev held back and, poker-faced, uttered in a low, controlled tone, "Who is welcoming me? is what I asked. And who are you?"

"I work with the IDF, Sir." The man was slightly taken aback, but quickly recovered. "And your welcome is from certain friends of yours in the Knesset and others who remember you well and owe you gratitude."

"Just so we understand each other. Now get him on the phone please." "What do you mean, Sir? That's impossible."

"Look," barked out Lebedev, towering over the other man, "he can see and hear us anyway. Now get him on the phone." The Israeli dithered and pretended to deliberate for a minute, but then dialled a number on his iPhone and spoke briefly before handing the instrument to the big man.

"Hela, Avi", he shouted. "What the fuck? The three Israelis looked impressed, and Betardo marvelled at the way people all over, often in authority, just accepted Pyotr and his often rough ways. He hadn't changed in the years that they had not seen each other. The policeman had been on secondment to the Spanish foreign service and had run into Lebedev in Algeria where the Russian was undefinedly associated with the military and with one of their most prolific generals. He remembered Pyotr punching the general joshingly to make a point, and wondered if he would also punch this Avi, whoever he was.

"Alocheim Shalom, brother, Tov, Toda. Sure I'll tell him." The conversation ended and he handed back the phone. "Thank you. Judah, you are Judah?" he said, telling more than asking the man. "We need a letter of free passage through West Bank signed by him. They can email it through and we can print it off in the terminal building no problem."

"I already have the letter here, Sir," said the man smiling drily, and producing an envelope which he handed to Pyotr.

"Thank you," said Pyotr. "Typical Israeli efficiency. Oh, and by the way, agent Aaron Peres, thank you for your time, but we will not be needing your help, and Chief Inspector Hassan. Arabic sounding name."

"Sephardic, Sir. We have not yet integrated any Arabs into the upper echelons of the INP, God forbid."

"Well, Inspector, many thanks for your welcome, and I am sure Chief Inspector Betardo and yourself will enjoy lunch

188

or supper together before he leaves the country." They all shook hands cordially, although the IDF man disconcertedly enquired as to the nature of their visit.

"We will just be interviewing some individuals, non-Israelis of course, about a situation which could well place our government in jeopardy, so discretion is of absolute necessity," Betardo informed him. "This is why I came with a built-in guide, not wishing to alert attention by being officially accompanied."

"Come on, Inspector," said Pyotr. "Good night, gentlemen." They started walking again toward the airport building blazing with light in the near distance. "Terminal three, police then customs and security and…"

"I don't understand. Why did we not let them fix us up? Why were we, or rather you, so unfriendly?"

"Because they are not friendly. All this friendliness is a sham. sure, some of the guys from the past may appreciate me still. We need to be discreet, and this lot will be breathing down our necks at every step."

"I had visions of Ben Gurion airport building being a bunch of Nissen huts," replied Betardo, interrupting his friend's tirade.

They approached the police passport booths together, where Betardo's passport was checked and stamped.

"Welcome to Israel, Chief Inspector. Have a fruitful stay." Pyotr had already been stamped, and together they made their way through customs and security with no delay.

"Don't change the subject on me, Señor Inspector," growled the Russian. "They are not at all friendly. I should know. I was one of them, one of the gang. It *was* a gang – of thugs."

On the thronging pavement outside the arrivals hall, Pyotr stopped and looked around, before pushing his way through the arriving passengers. He grabbed his colleague by the arm as he went.

"Please, Juan, just follow me and do as I say. Later I will explain."

They appeared out of the crowds, three men, and fell in with the two friends. The biggest man, with a large belly and a skull cap, came right up against them as they walked, jostled by the crowds. "Lebedev," he grunted. Betardo could smell the beer on his breath. The man looked at them and said again, "Lebedev."

"Da, shtoa?" (Yes what?) snarled Pyotr. The skull cap looked pointedly at him.

"Nikita Smith, that's the name I was told to say." He looked at Betardo and smiled. *"Gospodin"*

(Sir).

"Vcio harasho, karoche, pashlim," Pyotr answered curtly. (All OK, good. Let's cut and go.) *"Sherut,"* said Nikita.

"Da. OK," grunted Pyotr.

A white and yellow minibus (a Sherut) came up to the pavement and the two big men with Nikita shouldered the

190

crowds of people of all nationalities aside. One of them pulled the sliding door open and Pyotr pushed Juan towards it and climbed in after him. The others followed. The van took off fast but discreetly, and once clear of the airport stopped under an overhead road.

"Pete, tell me what is going on. What is all this cloak and dagger stuff?" "It's necessary, believe me."

Then a white and yellow cab came under the road.

"Let's go," barked Pyotr, and Betardo hurriedly followed him as they changed into the taxi.

"*Kak diela*? (How are you) said the driver. "Don't worry, they'll come, the watchers," he chuckled, "for the Cherut, which has a flat. That's what they'll find," he laughed. "They were hot on your tracks. I am Kolya." He looked over at Pyotr and offered a large hand. "I am the brother of Boris." Pyotr took his hand and shook it,

"Thank you. I am happy to see you. You don't look like him – you're an ugly bastard."

"He said you were friendly." They both laughed. "He also said you were a cunt." They laughed louder.

"Sorry to interrupt the niceties, but where are we going?"

"To Boris," said Pyotr. "Sorry, this is Chief Inspector Juan Betardo of the Spanish police," he said to the Russian, "and Boris is my friend from the old days, the Negev days, and this is his brother Nikolai, Kolya to friends. Good *Halacha* folk, old Kibbutzniks."

"Hello *Gospodin*," said the Russian.

"*Ochin priatna*," (pleased to meet you), replied the policeman. "Good Russian *ezyck*," (language) laughed Kolya.

"Halacha?" inquired the Spaniard.

"Halacha in this context means true Jew, mother Jewish," answered Pyotr. "They came to the Promised Land by right. The Law of Return amplifies this to grandparents, but the new government wants to alter it, saying they spend fortunes on immigrants who later leave."

"But Bringsten from Likud wants it to remain untouched. Someone called him the only pious Jew in Sodom," he laughed. "But it's true, you know. The rest of the government (to be) are unusual people, to say the least. They have needed to legislate to change the laws so they could govern."

"Anyway, we are Halacha, which also denotes Jewish law."

"Thank you," said Juan, "for your interesting explanations. Perhaps now you can give me an also interesting idea of our itinerary and what is happening. I arrived in Israel as an investigating authority, and in a short time seem to have converted into an illegal spy."

The two Russians guffawed loudly and Pyotr slapped the other man on his arm. "Spy!" he spluttered. "Spy."

Then the road signs started to announce Jerusalem, the West Bank, and so on, and after a sharp turn off the slip road from the motorway, the car drew into the courtyard of a small hotel. The signs, red and vividly visible, announced it: Hotel Kibbutz.

"Look, Juan, I need to fill you in on some stuff," said the big man as they climbed out of the car. "You go on, Kolya. We'll follow in a minute."

"Juan, I want you to know that I kept tabs on this suspected assassin of yours through my contacts, once you told me I was coming to Israel with you."

"I had expected some such. You are a free agent after all, and if I remember rightly, free of constraints by any nation or body."

"Yeah, well. Look, let me get to the point. I traced your man to Egypt and found who he spoke to, and who fixed him up for Gaza and stuff. After all, Gaza is not easy to visit. They, the people he is working with, are inside with Boris. We will meet them now."

"Fine by me, Dvai. Let's go," said the Spaniard, heading off out of the sultry Middle Eastern evening and up the few stairs to the air-conditioned lobby and reception of the hotel.

They were escorted to one of the hotel's conference rooms, where Kolya guided them in and a large man, nearly as big as Pyotr, greeted them with a strong handshake, a bearlike but brief embrace to Pyotr, and a smile. "I am Boris," he whispered to Betardo, and Pyotr smiled. Behind the two brothers at the conference table sat a large, fat man wearing a kippah and dressed in a white suit. Beside him, a girl and a smiling young man whispered to each other.

"*Buenas noches,*" said the young man, smiling as he stood up. The girl also stood, although the fat man stayed seated.

"*Muy buenas,*" replied Betardo with a small bow, first towards the young man and then to the girl. "*A sus pies. Que encanto de señorita, le felicito,* At your feet. What a charming young lady, I congratulate you" he uttered instinctively under his breath. The fat man scowled throughout the short exchange.

"Thank you, Sir," replied the girl. "I do understand Spanish. My name is Esther, and I am here accompanying my father on a visit to Israel and Palestine."

"Oh, I am sorry," said Betardo. "I am always talking aloud. Must be the pressure of work." "Or the wine on the plane," suggested Pyotr drily.

"We understand," cut in the fat man, "that you are from the Spanish police and that you are pursuing one of our doctors on suspicion of murder."

"Not exactly," retorted Betardo. "We just need to question him. He is only a suspect. To be truthful, we only have some limited circumstantial evidence against him."

"Question him? You mean you have come all the way from Spain just to question him, and you have nothing conclusive?"

" I have for many years followed my nose as a detective, and it works. I know it hardly sounds scientific, but what is a science after all if not a system of knowledge based on phenomena? Let's just say that I fancy him for this crime, fancy as in pigeons."

"There appears to be a certain affinity between you and your suspect, Sir," shouted the fat man. "You are both lunatics."

"Papa, papa, please," the girl implored him with gentle authority.

The young man raised his hands. "Please may we settle down. I do apologise to all. I should have affected the instructions when you arrived. This is Mr Moshe Abecassis and his daughter Esther. Moshe is the president in Egypt of the organisation known as Doctors of Love."

"We will travel together to the West Bank," said the fat man in his loud, forceful voice. "Why?" asked Pyotr.

"The West Bank is a big place full of checkpoints and military. You won't know where to start to look for the doctor, and you won't get far," explained the Jew. "Look here." He started getting excited again. "You are here to help the policeman. You look like a good man to know, but how do you think you will find him, the doctor? The crazy, wonderful doctor."

"We are worried about him," the girl joined in. "He is so special. The children were enchanted with him, but he is like a child."

"She danced with him all the night like she used to do with the children in the Strip before they killed her mother with the bombs," her father shouted. "Now she doesn't sleep. She wanted to follow him, but I forbade her." He was quiet for a few moments. "Now we are here and we will come with you. My brother Moses is a retired army major, you know. Very influential and had a sponsor, Palmach. He will get us through, otherwise, puff, there is a whole army deployed there."

"Ok," said Pyotr. He nodded to Boris and took him by the elbow for a confidential chat in a corner of the big room. "Do you know these people?"

"*Da*," the older man nodded. "I know him from way back, and his brother. I know you have made efforts to stay out of sight, but this is the best way. The brother, he has 'Ulpan, much hand', he was like a son to one of the old Haganah strike force people, you know, Palmach."

They met the retired major that evening in the bar of the hotel where they were to spend the night. He was very casually attired in jeans and a trendy T-shirt with a thin hoody jacket to cater for the cool of the evening. A quiet, attractive, unassuming man, some fifty-odd years of age, slim and tough, probably some sort of Uriah Heep (hidden strength) character who would only show his true self under duress. After all, he was a retired Israeli Army major, an army in which, by the sound of it, such a high rank needed to be earned. Moshe had assured Pyotr that he would look after them and that they could relax.

"Don't worry," the major smiled. "Tomorrow I will wear an olive green work uniform for travelling and will look more the part. After all, tradition has handed us this obligation."

Seeing that Pyotr and Betardo looked puzzled, he asked, "You do know who this guy is, don't you? The Moshe has told you?" He was cut off by an irate Moshe, who abruptly abandoned a conversation with his daughter Esther and the Catalan man Jordi. He took his brother's arm and pulled him out of the lounge.

"He didn't realise I am police. The Moshe, as he quaintly calls him, must have failed to inform him fully," Betardo suggested to Pyotr. "Strange, very strange. I was under the impression that O'Donovan, our fugitive, had never been in Israel, yet he is someone for them."

"Assuming he was referring to your fugitive when he said 'this guy'."

"Oh, he was," Betardo assured him. "I have no doubt. What puzzles me is his asking if we know who he is. Well, who is he? There's more to this than meets the eye. These guys seem to have some sort of alternative agenda to ours."

ANSAKI DEVOUT

.

Chapter Nineteen: Qualandia

From Qualandia to the north and to the south, they have built a wall of concrete blocks nine metres high and, where the walls cease, a multi-layered fence system, with three fence units with pyramid-shaped stacks of barbed wire on the two outer fences and a lighter-weight one with intrusion detection equipment in the middle; an anti-vehicle ditch; patrol roads on both sides; and a smooth strip of sand for "intrusion tracking".

As you drive on a sunny day through the Palestine countryside it hits you that they have built it not inside the country that it purports to defend but in Palestine. It was never for defence at all, but the start of the big steal, the rape of Palestine and her children using the massive financial aid arriving faithfully each year from the US.

The Cherut weaves its way through cars and people. Pete, Betardo, Moshe, Esther, and Geordie. Colia is driving and the Major, Moshe's brother, Esther's uncle, sits in the front passenger seat.

"Go straight up to the front, to the barrier. Go."

"But he's waving me down," protests Kolya. The soldier – a girl – is starting to unstrap her gun off her shoulder to bring the weapon to bear.

"Go," says the Major as he waves some sort of insignia out of the window and suddenly screams out at the soldiers in

Hebrew. An officer has seen and heard the interchange and shouted orders to them. They shoulder their guns in response and wave them on. The minibus stops at the barrier and the waiting officer salutes and questioningly indicates the people in the Cherut with a sweep of his hand. There is an interchange of Hebrew, and the Major utters the words "My party." The barrier goes up and the officer salutes, the Major salutes back, and they are in the West Bank.

"Now they are calling me," says the Major and looks back at Pete. "I won't answer. Enough that they know it's me." Then he smiled. "I am sure they know it's you also, Russian." Pete did not reply.

Kolya bursts out laughing once they are well clear.

"My quickest crossing ever, no visas, no passports, then he waves his hand in the air splendidly and says 'My party'." A hesitant chuckle comes from the rear of the bus.

"Probably they are curious, Russian," he says, again looking at Pete. "They are kicking it around between them, maybe chuckling. You know who, you know them from long ago. Please relax, though," says the Major. "We have an hour or two to travel. Follow the signs to Nablus, and expect frequent controls. Between fixed and flying checkpoints there must be over five hundred in the whole West Bank."

"That is one hell of a lot. How do the people live?" asks Pete.

The Major just shrugged his shoulders. "I am retired, thank God."

They travel through the morning, flying past checkpoints or being diverted, the Major waving his insignia lavishly out of the window, but they are probably all aware of who he is and of his presence.

"This is an army," says Pete, "a real army of occupation."

And of destruction, dissuasion," says Kolya. "They kill, kidnap, destroy all essential infrastructure so that a village, any village, cannot survive. They bulldoze whole areas and build their settlements."

"And the children," says Esther, "are the real target. The settlers, who are also an armed force as numerous as the soldiers if not more, spearhead the attack. And then the soldiers will take children at random, small children, beat them, and make them crawl on their knees to the checkpoints."

"Don't go on," says her father. "It will just break you. Let's just go and do what we are doing. Let us find your friend the crazy man."

They are close to Nablus.

"A flying control. They are waving us down. Stop the van slowly," orders the Major.

"Major," the soldier salutes. "Turn off next junction. The first village is where your doctor is. He is making trouble. We are working Nablus and surrounding areas, clear up operations. Be careful – lots of activity."

ANSAKI DEVOUT

Chapter Twenty:
Alarico Hoists The Flag

"My name is Alarico O'Donovan de Medinacheli. I am Spanish, a doctor, and the first son of an old family.

"If I tire, forgive me, as I was recently shot in the stomach by the apartheid nation of Israel for the crime of shielding some young kids, thinking the soldiers, the killers, would respect me in my medical doctor's garb and the Spanish flag I had held in front of myself. When I fell wounded some children tried to drag me away to safety. A soldier stamped his boot on my hand to stop them, and I screamed. This much I am told, as I lost and regained consciousness many times. I am told that they shot me because they believed I was Palestinian.

"I am accused or suspected of the murder of an American in Spain. They have come," he gestured with his chin, "the police, to take me back to Spain. I did not commit the murder but I read the statement or epistle confession in which the assassin justifies his actions. After what I have seen and experienced in Palestine, in Gaza, and later in the West Bank, I can only say that this assassin is right."

"Cross-C Digital News. Mr O'Donovan, are you saying you would have killed the Senator yourself?"

The Spanish police officer, Juan Betardo, stood up.

"I am Chief Inspector Juan Betardo of the Spanish Judicial Police, and Mr. O'Donovan is here in my custody. He came to the Gaza Strip to work with the children and I followed to arrest him on suspicion of murder.

"We are aware of who you all are. Only a dozen press entities have been allowed in on Mr. O'Donovan's insistence, and because this is a relatively small hall. This is a privilege accorded to you, as half the world's press is out there and they are not party to this gathering. They have not been invited. Mr. O'Donovan just wishes to make a statement and does not wish to reply to questions. Mr O'Donovan has signed a notarised document declaring his innocence and agreeing to take a lie detector test on his return to Spain, in return for which we have acceded to the press conference. Furthermore, Mr O'Donovan is very weak due to blood loss caused by the initial impossibility of ambulances reaching the scene where he was shot whilst trying to shield young children from Israeli bullets. The ambulances were forcibly prevented from coming by Israeli troops who do this in the hope that the victim, their victim, will bleed to death.

"Are you making an official statement, Chief Inspector? Is this it?"

"I am speaking as a witness, as a human being. I saw what went on and would further add that I find it deplorable that these so-called soldiers shoot people in the offhanded and slap-happy fashion in which they do, aiming for the stomach, something that appears to be policy amongst them.

"I come from a democratic country where this sort of dirty thing does not occur, and where people are allowed to stand up and say the truth about what happened. I deplore the behaviour of these employees of the Israeli government and will make official representations to my superiors on my return, in the hope that this is brought before the European Parliament and the United Nations, for all the good it may do.

" I am grateful to the Jordanian authorities and army who made no problem at all in allowing us to enter the country at the Allenby Bridge crossing, provided an effective escort, led us to the hospital, and are now running a control to protect me and my party.

"Perhaps you would continue now, Mr O'Donovan. We trust you will be afforded the courtesy of no further interruptions."

"Thank you, Juan, Inspector," replied the man in the bed, shaking his head as if to clear it. May I say that as an arresting officer, Inspector Betardo and his team have been human, very human, towards me, their suspect. The Inspector has a knowledge, a personal brushing with evil, though it be transcended through the windows of time, but I have perceived during our conversations that it has touched him irremediably; made him human. Juan Betardo's grandparents met on the road of the Desbandada, a ferocious and terrific attack by the fascist rebel army of Spain, under the command of the unmentionable Queipo de Llano on fifteen thousand fleeing refugee families; five thousand perished.

"That was in nineteen thirty-seven, 1937, but this is today. In the present time, two hundred Palestinian people have been killed by Israel in the year 2022 alone, including fifty children. This is no war, no conflict; no, this is murder, and complicit in what is happening is every politician who has been involved, every willing soldier, every general, policeman or woman, interrogator, torturer, demolition crew of legitimate houses, bomber pilots who have murdered the innocent with no qualms, newspaper people who have distorted or blocked the truth. Europe and America as well as all those nations who have in any way supported, backed, and participated in this progressive genocide, this apartheid, are as responsible as the actual bombers and shooters. This filthy genocidal repression of the people of Palestine has been going on since well after the end of World War two.

"The list of peoples put into dire crises such as in Palestine is interminable. In every country and in every activity in the world, some people ignore their inner voice, if indeed they have one at all. We know that those with no conscience are psychopaths; but how many of these are self-taught, self-induced for the sake of power, material gain, or carnal desire?"

He groans loudly, and the doctor shakes his head toward Betardo, who nods. The nurse, a small, smiling woman, gives him water and strokes his head. She whispers in his ear words that have no meaning to him, but she utters them because she must, because she has been cast under his spell. To her, he is a child needing love. Then she checks the tubes feeding blood and fluid to his ravaged body.

Betardo asks him to stop, and he smiles back at him, weakly reasoning, "Please, Chief Inspector, I am not finished."

The policeman nods, and the wounded man continues with his monologue. His voice is weak, and the microphone held by one of the two Spanish reporters is brought closer.

"Ansaki – this is the name our Sotogrande assassin has given himself and all those that may follow him. He defines his would-be fellow killers as sanitisers, removers of evil, surgeons cutting out and purging cancers. He calls them Angels, Saints, and Killers, hence the word derived from that: AN.SA.KI. But even if many good, clean, idealistic people were inspired to participate, there would perhaps also be complete bodies of people, of individuals with less just inclinations and agendas climbing onto the bandwagon. Yes, say I, but there would always be new, clean, pure Ansaki emerging from the shadows to remove these impure leeches.

"These pure Ansaki would always be totally secretive. In secrecy lies purity. Their only solace, true friend, conversant and confessor would be God, their own God."

The wounded man's voice is raised and he shouts, "God, yes, God is watching us, observing, he sees all. Even Halachic law, the very Torah, tells you that if someone comes to kill you and your brothers then rise up and kill

207

him, that it is just. For how long do we expect the Palestinians and the Yemeni to have genocides imposed upon them? To have the blood of their innocents in their thousand flow in rivers of red?

"And who are guilty?" Again he shouts, his voice trembling with passion.

"This, the very Ansaki will in their wisdom define. They will remove presidents and vice presidents, generals, politicians who steal and do not love their state, media people who block or do not allow the truth to be propagated, people who commit crimes against children, and those who fly in the face of common law passed to protect children, or help to distort or change such laws. They will remove evil soldiers, wanton killers, those who thieve off the needy, and corrupt billionaires who refuse to use their wealth for the well-being of their brothers and to pay morally legitimate taxes.

"And our planet, our beautiful home. There will be Ansaki who will set their sights on those politicians, business people, or individuals who are threatening the well-being of the planet. We should all look after this piece of the universe that gives us so much, and yet the whole process we have in place today is geared up to enrich part of our populace at the expense of the destruction of our physical world.

"Stop him, stop him now," whispers the Jordanian doctor to Betardo. "Look at him. What's driving him? He's practically in a catatonic state. It's impossible that he should be here pronouncing this incredibly long declaration from memory. Look at him – he's sitting up rigidly. His eyes are not focussing."

"We're stopping this," barks Betardo.

"Let him finish," snaps the attractive girl who is still holding the microphone to the mouth of the wounded man. The other Spanish girl holds the nurse and doctor aside by not moving, despite their attempts to get to the patient.

"I expect that the Ansaki will target thousands, even hundreds of thousands of individuals, every single person involved in industries that are detrimental to the health of Mother Earth. CEOs of irresponsible oil companies, coal and mining companies, logging entities, politicians, bankers, financiers, rulers of countries, and manipulators for bad ends, of which, due to the social media phenomenon, there are so many stirring the pots of war, plague and the myriad other unclean issues out of which they may draw an immoral dividend. The list will go on without end until the evil and destructive practices cease altogether and the epithet God- fearing', which has of late become so rarely applicable to persons in power, will be strengthened by the new appendage, Ansaki-fearing.

His words are cut off by the interference of Jordanian police officers, who have been signalled by Betardo. They pull the girls and the microphone away, and allow the doctor to attend to the bedridden man. The press people's cameras and video cameras, all of which had pushed their way forward during the spectacle, are pushed back, and in the ensuing commotion, Pete shoulders people away in order to get to a crying Esther and her father Moshe.

"That was not the man I met in Egypt," shouted Moshe to Pete in a not-to-be-quietened tone. "This man is magnificent. He is so magnificent, God bless him, he is like a man possessed. He said it all, he said all that needed to be said to the world. This was his moment and he knew it. Now he can go away and die. He has done his work."

"Stop it, Papa, stop it. He will not die. Why should he die just because he is the first truly good man you have ever met?"

"But he was the man who came to your offices in Egypt?" asked Betardo with a frown.

"Yes, of course, he is. Only he has changed. Gaza has made him older and so strong. In Egypt he was a fool; here, now, he seems like a different man. I am so proud to have been instrumental in bringing him here."

"We can't leave this place for a while," said one of the two Spanish girls who joined them accompanied by their crew. The younger, fiery one who had handled the microphone, Delaisandra, interrupted their conversation.

"The world will listen? The world already knows. He knows that they, the world, know about the Palestine atrocities, yes, but he is telling them that the Ansaki are here and that the murders in every country, in every single part of the world, will multiply. That was his message. I think he was telling them to be afraid. Also, he was inviting all those thousands of inspired persons, hundreds of thousands, to seek justice, actively."

"Do you mean by murdering prominent people?"

"You heard him speak. Governments, not all but many all over the world, and not just the governments, are murdering people in their thousands daily, officially."

"But two wrongs don't make a right."

"You heard him, for him it's not wrong, it's a moral obligation, a saintly mission, an amputation I think is the word he used."

"Who used? But he said he is not the Sotogrande assassin."

" Yes, so he did, but he also said that seeing what goes on in Palestine firsthand, has made him believe that the assassin is right."

"And will his words get out?" asked Pete. "Everything seems so controlled these days."

Delaisandra winked at him. Unknown to all, Pete was the one who had contacted them. She and her colleague Rocio were to jet over from Malaga with a full press crew.

"Yes, sir," she said. "It's already in Spain being prepared for immediate broadcast by the main press outfits we're sponsored by. It will be seen in every home in every country in the world.

ANSAKI DEVOUT

Chapter Twenty-One:
The Prodigal Son

As just a tiny dot in the brightest blue sky, the aircraft appeared. It came out of the glaring afternoon from the direction of Madrid and the north, and of Europe. Before touching down at the Spanish military airbase of Torrejon de Ardoz for refuelling it had overflown Israel, Greece, and the Aegean, and Italy and the Mediterranean. It had not been there seconds before, just a black dot growing rapidly, and then it was three black dots. The images were being seen all over Spain by millions of people, probably even by billions all over the world. Then the plane could be seen a little more clearly; preceding and following it were two Spanish Eurofighter Typhoons, which would be seen to be carrying the insignia, "Ejercito del aire y del espacio, Reino de España".

Andalucia awaits. Toreadors, and matadors, touched by the hot afternoon sun and bearing their *capotes* (capes) and *espadas* (swords), embarked on their *faenas* (struggle) to bring the occasion to its finale with the p*untilla* (killing knife) to ensure the death, the end of the agony. None of them in all the glory of their *trajes de luces(glittering costumes)* and *salidas por la puerta grande(emergence from the ring after the corrida, carried by the crowd through the main gates)* have ever enjoyed the incredible popularity and acclaim proffered today at Malaga Airport, the unexpected support for the man the crowds believe to

213

be on the incoming aircraft. Vans of all descriptions from every TV station in Spain and France, and others from Germany, Scandinavia, and all over Europe, each with their distinctive logo stamped on roof and doors, are everywhere.

The whole airport complex is jammed with vehicles and dense crowds. All-access roads are full of unmoving traffic. The Guardia Civil de Trafico have closed them off and are vigorously yet ineffectively waving on motorway traffic that has slowed to nearly a halt. Hundreds of cars have come off onto the hard shoulder for kilometres along the highway.

What has motivated so many to come? Maybe the fact that he is Spanish, or perhaps just because he is real and has touched so many deep down. Yet the crowds are aware that they are unlikely to catch even a glimpse of the traveller as it has been made clear by the authorities on the news and on every social media channel that the individual is under arrest and will be transferred directly from the plane to the military base beside the runway, which is a shared facility between the commercial and the military. But they have come in such immense numbers to be a part of the arrival of the plane carrying this unusual prisoner. They have heard and seen him on multiple ill-prepared video recordings of a chaotic scene in the West Bank of occupied Jerusalem. He is holding up a Spanish flag with his left hand, and with his right is pushing some children behind him. They heard his screaming and could make out the words, barely audible because of the racket, "They are only kids, don't shoot," and then, as the soldiers must have started taking aim, *"Cobardes, hijos de puta."* Then he crumples up as they shoot him, in the belly, we later learn. The children try to drag him away, but a soldier stamps on his hand to stop them, and other soldiers set about the children, punching and kicking them. Then someone comes running up and intervenes, shouting and pushing the soldiers aside, an officer by the looks of it, must be someone well known as the soldiers pull back. Then other people run forward, a Jewish man, a woman, and some others, the man is also screaming in Hebrew.

Then the officer is shouting at the soldiers. This on yet another video; in fact, all this is a composite of many recordings, edited into the best possible record of the events. There is an ambulance, its lights flashing, a Palestinian ambulance; the soldiers have been holding it back at gunpoint as it tries to get through. Then the video cuts off.

This is what the people of Spain, and indeed the world, have been seeing flashing on their TVs and computers: this short but highly emotive composite video, and then, a day later, they see the victim of the shooter, the Spanish valiant speaking from his hospital bed, now in Amman in neighbouring Jordan. They are told he is a suspect in the murder of the American Senator and possibly the person emitting highly provocative and illegal press releases all over the world, inciting others to do as he has done. From his bed, despite his wounds and practically in a trance, he tells people what happened and what is happening over the frontier, and that the world has not been told of the murders of so many children over so many years.

The plane is now close and has headed out to sea to prepare its approach for Malaga Airport. The bright sunlight is reflected in a blinding set of flashes off its wings as it banks over the Mediterranean and lines up to land. The escorting jet fighters still hover above, awaiting clearance to come in, and the sound of their engines combines with that of the large Fuerzas del Aire personnel carrier as it touches down, the pilot downs flaps and the jet engines go into reverse. The resulting roar is close to deafening for those standing closest to the perimeter fence.

The crowds wait silently as the aircraft taxis to the military side of the airport, and an ambulance, lights flashing, and other vehicles drive up to the now stationary plane. In the distance, the plane's rear ramp can be seen lowering, and then a group of white-coated medics, military personnel, and civilians escort a wheeled stretcher as it descends onto the tarmac. A muted roar goes up, building in intensity with car klaxons, wolf whistles, and people clapping and shouting, perhaps fifty or sixty thousand strong. They can minutely see the figure on the stretcher raise an arm as if in gratitude or recognition, and the shouting increases to a crescendo, reaching the impossible in its intensity. Then the stretcher enters the waiting ambulance and the moment is passed, the traffic starts to move and the crowds dissolve. But they had been there, they had welcomed him on his return, and they had been witnesses.

Chapter Twenty-Two:
Jihad

"Let me tell you a story, Juan. In or around 1985, the war for Afghanistan was on. As you may know, the Pakistani city of Peshawar was a major staging point for the war, as it was to here that thousands of Muslim men from all around the globe were flocking to fight their holy Jihad (struggle) against the Russian invaders of neighbouring Afghanistan.

Close to Peshawar is a fortress named Bandabar, where the Pakistani army in liaison with the CIA had imprisoned a selection of Russian high-security prisoners together with some Afghans and others unknown. A contact, a very special one-off contact within Pakistani army security, has given us a verbal report about one man, a Muslim, a Moroccan known as Sidi Mohamed. This guy was a sort of Lone Ranger who conducted his own private Jihad but hear this. His targets were not just Russians, no sir, this fellow was after any offender against children. Well, he shot Russians, he shot Afghans, Mujahideens, and CAA covert people working on the ground. Then, he told us, although there is nothing in US military records to bear it out, that a wounded CAA spook was coptered into Peshawar. Our contact tells us quite specifically that he was a target or hit made by the secretive Sidi Mohamed. He, our contact knows because he was hot on Mohamed's trail at the time. The CAA spook, the victim, was a soldier bearing the same name as our deceased of the Sotogrande shooting, the Senator, Senator Smith.

Jose Garcia was seated at a desk on the raised dais at the Policia Nacional barracks in Malaga. With him, also sitting around desks casually and drinking tea, were Juan Betardo and Laura Galvez Diaz, Chief Inspector of the Policia Nacional. A policewoman on an adjacent desk was typing in information at a fast speed as Laura instructed her, and bringing up images on one of the large screens facing them. The rest of the hall was deserted and the only lights were at the front raised area and the access corridor.

"The plot thickens," remarked Betardo with a mock gloomy expression. "I suppose you're after shooting down my candidate for the part of assassin?" Garcia just smiled and waved an instructive finger at Laura and her assistant.

Pictures flashed up showing various damaged buildings, and then a man, a younger-looking version of the man they all recognised as Senator Smith.

"He went further, did our contact. He sent us this: this photo was taken there in Peshawar, I imagine by Pakistani army people keeping track of US visitors. Now that's him 1985, our Senator himself, in Peshawar. The wounded man was his son," carried on Garcia, "the wounded soldier. And the most mysterious part is that there is no record as to what outfit the son was with and no explanation as to how he was wounded."

And here's the punchline. A special group was set up, probably on the insistence of Senator Smith. Made up of

Pashtuni, military, and CAA. They went in and with the help of some Mujahideen rounded up the Lone Ranger, Sidi Mohamed, and brought him out. He had been betrayed by some top tribal guy, some Mujahideen chieftain, who had been his friend – Suleiman Rasul Kamatki was his name. Mohamed was then imprisoned in the fortress of Bandabar, but then there was this uprising and all the prisoners were killed.

"So what then, Jose? What have you got? Tell us – don't drag it out as usual."

"After your little Israeli pilgrimage you can talk, Roberto, or is that me?" They smiled at each other.

"They never found his body. Buuuut," Garcia went on, after a dramatic pause. "He had a son. The boy we know lots about because of the Moroccans, specifically the DST, Direccion de Surveillance du Territoire. After 2005 it became the DGST, just in case you want to go looking it up."

"No, no, please do continue with your fascinating narrative, Q. I'm quite eager to see where it's all going."

"Well the DST kept tabs on the boy and the family of Sidi Mohamed for all the time he was abroad. You see he, Sidi Mohamed, developed this incredible reputation amongst the hardened tribes of mountain men of the Atlas. That's why they called him Sidi, Sidi means saint, to them he was a great hero fighting for Allah. So if you consider, the boy, who was born just after Sidi Mohamed departed for Peshawar, would today be 38 years old. Well, the

Moroccans tell us that the boy grew up to a very great extent emulating his father. He was a total loner and also went to the Madrasah in Marrakech where he studied the Koranic and Sufi texts before returning to, IDraren Draren. That's what the High Mountains people call the place, Mountains of Mountains. And then he travelled out of Morocco to, guess where now, Peshawar, and disappeared. The Pakistanis surmise that he trained with the Taliban or Al Quaeda in all aspects of hidden warfare, and it appears he became quite adept.

"We are told that someone got at Suleiman Rasul Kamatki, you know the old warlord involved in Sidi Mohamed's capture, this was sometime around 2015. He was killed with a bullet to the back of the neck, executioner style, and had a copy of the sacred book, the Holy Koran with him as he died. Thereafter the Pakistanis, Americans, Pashtunis, and Afghans suffered a spate of similar killings on both sides of the border, always with a Holy Koran. The killer probably made the victim say his prayers. The victims were generally high-ups, politicians and army generals or colonels, warlords or leaders, and invariably had a reputation for killing young people or children. He was a really scary, spooky killer, and many thought that he didn't really exist, that he was an avenging spirit.

"People thinking they were targeted by him would try to lock themselves away under guard in a remote spot, and yet they would be found dead. They call him Sidi Hamou, assuming that he is the boy, the son of Sidi Mohamed."

"Sooooo!" barked a bored Juan Betardo, putting a hand up to his mouth to stifle a yawn. "So where is this Sidi Hamou? Is he our man?"

"We don't know," answered Laura. "Our Pakistani contact believes it well could be. What we do know is that the language they speak in that part of the world ranges between Pashko, Hindko, Urdu, Ossetic, and some Russian. Now as far as we know such a range is rare in this part of the world, here in Malaga. Yes, we are very cosmopolitan, but this sort of mix we had never heard before. So when by a stroke of luck a Pakistani waiter wishing to ingratiate himself with the authority called into the Guardia Station in Estepona something clicked. He's a waiter at the beach club restaurant. He had a group of four very unsavoury-looking big individuals eat in the restaurant. He says they spoke in Pashko, Urdu, bits of Russian, and Hindko. He says that they spoke in English and Pashko, but when one of them did not understand something it was said again in his own language."

The Guardia Civil captain again took up the explanation.

"We were fortunate that he, the waiter, used the security camera to take a secret picture of them. Again my friend Juan, thank you for your patience. We believe that there could possibly be a connection between these individuals and the disappeared Sidi Hamou."

"You mean," asked Juan, "that he, Sidi Hamou, is in Spain and that he is our Sotogrande killer?"

"Well," replied Garcia, "perhaps he knew things about this deceased Senator and his son that we do not and that this may have been his motive in the assassination."

"Far-fetched but feasible," added Laura, "but it's a potential suspect. God knows we need a break on this case unless, of course, your doctor fails the lie detector test."

"He won't," replied Juan, "but I still have faith in him being our killer." "Faith is hardly the word."

"Perhaps so," replied Juan.

"So," said Garcia, "we need to interview these individuals but have had no luck so far in locating three of them. There is only one of them who we know, and we have already brought him in. Please may we have the photo up on the screen?"

They looked up at the large screen as the image appeared, a larger-than-life impression showing four men sitting around a table laden with food and wine. One of them was expressively talking while two were busy using their cutlery, and a fourth was sitting back expansively holding his wine goblet and listening.

"Shit," spat out Betardo. "Shit."

"Looks very like your friend Pete," said Garcia icily.

"Yes it's Pete, Jose, you know it bloody is. It was stated quite clearly from the onset if you care to check out the minutes for our first Taskforce meeting that he and his companions, as appeared on our bike concentration video, were all potential suspects. But what the hell is the problem here? At this moment in time, all we know is that he is having a meal with a group of guys who speak languages. I hope you've, brought him in, politely. Come to think of it, when we spoke to Pete in the first place he told us that he was having lunch with three guys on the day and time of the shooting."

"Yes, of course, we have gone after him with great courtesy. After all, we are aware of your friendship and your Israel trip together. I sent a car with three Civiles just in case he made a run for it. he is a very large man after all."

"Thinking about it, actually I doubt whether they'll be successful in inviting him in. Damn it, Jose, it is a rather clumsy way to go about things given the personage involved. You could've just asked me. A call would have done the trick."

The Guardia Civil captain's phone shrilled. He left the room to reply after glancing at the screen. Betardo looked at Laura, and Laura looked back. They could hear the captain in the corridor screaming into his phone.

"I think they've lost him," she smiled. Betardo had that sort of effect on most people. He just smiled some more and winked at her as Garcia stormed back into the room.

The captain resumed his seat.

"Don't worry," said Juan. "He'll call me and I'll apologise on your behalf."

"Apologise? Apologise? I said to them, just say that Captain Garcia would like to talk to you. He said fine, just one moment, please. And he's gone, the reception didn't see him go, nobody saw him go."

Betardo's phone rang.

"It's him, Pete. Do you want to apologise? Hello Pete, sorry mate. Just put you on loudspeaker so friends can listen in."

"Sure, no problem. What idiot sent the goons? Three to ask a guy around for a chat, three big guys."

"Sorry, Pete. He apologises."

"Ok, so you want a meet, him and you and me, that's it. Anyone else I disappear again, and by the way, what the fuck does he want?"

"We need your help with some guys you had lunch with in some beach club."

"Why doesn't he check it out with his people in Madrid for starters? I'll be in touch." The phone rang off.

"What's he mean about Madrid?"

"No idea, but I have a feeling you're about to get egg all over your face."

Chapter Twenty-Three: Coin

A hot afternoon. The coast lies twenty kilometres behind them. Just Pete, Betardo and Garcia, no driver. Fields on either side of the narrow track, pomegranates brilliant red gracing green bushes in the sun, persimmons, avocados. The track rises over the crest of a gradient and the crops still crowd the jeep as it makes its bumpy way. The town of Coin fell back a while ago when they left the tarmac. They labour over the brow of the incline and motor down toward a narrow concrete bridge carrying one carriageway and a circular ceramic tube of vehicle diameter right across the river, except that it's dry.

"Rio Pereilha," says Betardo. "Soon the Grande will appear and we will be close."

The Guardia Civil captain is driving, silently. He asks, as if out of the blue, although it's what they are all wondering: "Why so much secrecy, after all? They are here in Spain as guests of our government and the Guardia Civil."

"We don't know," Pete answers drily. "Perhaps they are afraid, and not of the Spanish authority. These people, only today, work for Pakistani army security and presumably the CIA. When I knew them in Afghanistan they worked for us, for Russian army intelligence. I agreed to meet them when they contacted me as I was interested to learn what they were doing here."

"And what did they say?"

There is a long silence from Pete. He is not angry at the pettiness of the captain's actions, only wary. Now he knows the animal. To him, the Guardia Civil Officer is irritable like a wasp. Pete will weigh his words.

"They told me nothing. I know them. I know the personality of such people. They were with Russian military intel in Afghanistan, and now they are Pakistani army. So who are they really? Who payrolls the Pakistanis?"

Another rise, a plain, the flood plain of a meandering river. The jeep's tyres scrunch loudly. Clumps of tall, boughy eucalyptus all over, their roots holding the banks together. A light blue sky, quite luminous with large white clouds scudding across, seemingly changing direction and going back on themselves again and again. Pungent herbal smells and aromas carry in the slight breeze and enhance the lethargy of the afternoon. The river is alive, with various separate streams running along her bed. Hordes of frogs singing their weird refrain. They lock up their vehicle and wait.

"How will they come?" They hear far-off buzzing.

"Bikes, it seems," Betardo answers his own question. "I was thinking maybe horses."

They come bursting out of the thickets on the other side of the small single-car bridge that crosses the Rio. The riders are young-seeming and masked, riding four powerful BMW mountain bikes built for the toughest terrain. They scrunch to a gravelly halt on the other side of the bridge and one of them signals for them to go over. Pete leads and greets the riders. They converse, and Pete selects one who has put his bike on its stand. He gets behind the machine and lifts the rider off it by the shoulders. He sets him down gracefully on the pillion of the neighbouring one. All in one rapid movement, and then he is on the vacant bike revving up. He motions to Betardo and Garcia to climb onto the passenger seats of the remaining bikes. Nobody opposes him. Nobody even objects. Pete signals and the bikes plunge again into the thickets from whence they have come. After a few minutes of driving crazily through trees and along footpaths through cereal fields, the lead bike comes to a halt.

"We must scan you for all of our protection," shouts one of the lads, and proceeds with an antenna-like instrument.

"And the drones following us?" asks Pete. "They are ours," answers the man.

"There was an alien drone, probably police," puts in another rider, "but it came to an unpleasant end." They all laugh.

The trail continues endlessly. It seems purposely long to confuse the visitors. Another river crossing, perhaps the Pereilha again, then a very steep incline, the passengers hanging on grimly. Both police officers are fit – many hours working out in the police gym. Finally a descent into a glade-like place, again close to water, evident by virtue of an abundance, a forest of very tall reeds which sway in the light breeze. They follow the beaten path among the reeds to eventually emerge onto a cleared area, a sort of secretive hidden enclave, and a building.

"It's an old church."

"Riddled with bullet holes," says Betardo. "Civil War residue, over eighty years old. Must be where *Regulares*, Moroccan troops from Franco's army, chased down the communists from the town. The poor bastards probably holed up here, and here the *regulares* found them. Of course, we don't know what the guys did if they had killed off priests or rich people in the Pueblo. Civil war is so evil. So many years and it's still here untouched," he says in a hushed, respectful voice, and all are quiet. Their reverie is broken by one of the men.

"Shall we go in? They are waiting."

Inside, a schoolroom that was, with many children's desks, wood benches, a large blackboard, wood, and peeling cork boards nailed to some walls, and old rubbished books littered in piles everywhere. Betardo stops to pick one up, its pages withered with age and mildew.

"Nineteen fifty-two, just after the end of the war." Squinting at the cover in the gloom.

"Indeed," answers a voice from the shadows in what would have been the vestry. Three men emerge.

"After the war so much had been destroyed, so few buildings left, so little food. This church was in a large private estate and a priest set up a shelter here to try to return a semblance of order and normality to so many distraught and hopeless kids. Then he started to teach, and as the town slowly reorganised it became more of a school. That was a long time ago. The priest was my uncle. I am Aparicio with CNI, intelligence." He casually shows them a shield.

Pete greets the foreigners in some unknown tongue, after which they go into English. "What happened to your colleague?" Again the men lapse into Urdu.

"It seems," said Pete, "that the third member of their party has disappeared. Then they were brought here by their counterparts in Spanish Military Intelligence when it was suspected that they also were under threat."

"So," says Betardo irately, "what agencies and with whom are we dealing here, please?"

"Well," put in Aparicio, "it was CIFAS, Spanish Military Intelligence to begin with. Our friends here are from military intelligence in Pakistan. But we are CNI, Spanish Intelligence. It was passed to us as Morocco is involved. It appears that the loose cannon, a Moroccan national who was active as a terrorist in Pakistan and on the border with Afghanistan, may be here. Hence the appearance on the scene of our friends from Pakistan, whom we invited to come to Spain in the hope that they will aid us in identifying him, but it appears that he identified them first, leading to the disappearance of one of them. This individual is highly dangerous and very elusive. They call him Sidi Hamou and many believe he does not exist, but he does."

"Yes, replied Garcia, we know of Sidi Hamou. We were in touch with the DST in Rabat. You see, Sidi Hamou's father had some sort of connection with our dead Senator and his son in or around 1985, and he, the Senator, was, we suspect, instrumental in Hamou's father being captured and killed. We believe that Sidi Hamou embarked on a revenge killing spree in 2015, starting with the murder of Suleiman Rasul Katmatki, a traitor who betrayed his late father, and that now in 2023 he has come to Spain and has murdered the Senator for his part in whatever happened to his father."

"You're Garcia. Captain Guardia Civil? We spoke about the rifle." "What rifle?" butts in Betardo, frowning.

"The murder weapon," says Aparicio. "I thought you fellows worked together?"

"Yes, I am Captain Jose Garcia of the Guardia Civil. We sent the rifle to you yesterday evening with one of our agents. It is a murder weapon indeed, the weapon used to murder the Israeli Colonel Ruben Misrahi, our ballistics people tell us, and not the Senator, but we believe it will turn out to be the same hitman for both targets using different weapons. When we ran the prints nothing matched any of the likelies off our total database, or Interpol's for that matter. Nothing at all."

"We always prefer to see the actual weapon," replied Aparicio. "Immediately we receive the gun, our counterparts in Pakistan and Morocco will receive the prints from us and run them. See what they come up with."

Ok, we're done here," interjects Betardo with a face like thunder. "Thank you, Aparicio, gentlemen." He strides out of the chapel with Pete in tow and jumps onto a bike pillion. Pete kicks her engine, throttles her viciously, and they take off into the passage through the reeds. They arrive at the second bridge without mishap.

"You are one incredible pathfinder Pete," said Betardo.

"Naw, they ran us around all over the place to confuse us, but I've been at the game for long enough," he laughs. "I don't get lost easily."

They roar past the car in which they had come where it sits morosely on the river gravel, cross the first river, the Pereilha, and set off through the fields.

"Shall we wait for Captain Garcia?" enquires Pete.

"Fuck Captain Garcia," answers Betardo with a grin. "Let's go steal some fruit."

Persimmons, of the chalky, very sweet variety are their first sampling, very juicy and sticky. Young sweetcorn, tender and succulent. An old man comes out of the bushes wielding a stick.

"Thieves! The corn ears are for my *burra*." So they run.

Young ripe avocados. "Ripe on the tree. They are here specially for us, Pete. Look, I have my pocket knife. Shame we didn't bring salt, we have a lemon tree here."

He plucks four large avocados with brown-green corrugated skin and proceeds to slice two of the fruits down the middle and extract the massive stone.

"I make some incisions along the meat and now squeeze the lemon juice into it."

They sit on the ledge beside the irrigation canal that waters the fields, the sun hot but pleasant, is made gentle by occasional clouds.

"Country towns in rural areas of Andalucia still have a Mayor of the Water, an elected official responsible for the allocation of the distribution of the water for irrigation. This canal we are washing our sticky hands and faces in is part of a huge network covering the whole area. This farmer, for example, receives water along the bypass canal at certain hours each day. He removes this wooden slat that serves as a dam and the water fills up all his canals so that the fields soak for an hour or whatever his allocated time is. They tell me that the system has been in place since Moorish times."

"He's mistaken, you know." "Pardon?" said Pete questioningly.

"Your man Garcia, the captain, he thinks he's got the upper hand because he kept the discovery of the rifle from me, but he's very wrong."

"All he said back there — his theories sound perfectly feasible to me," answered Pete, "although the man is out of order. Sounds like he's envious or something."

"No, that doesn't matter to me. Petty jealousies don't bother me. No, I'm just saying that he's wrong. Sidi Hamou did not murder our Senator, and after all the prime drive for our task force is to establish who did kill the Senator."

And as an afterthought: "In fact, we don't even know yet if Sidi Hamou murdered Misrahi. It's all wishful conjecture. No, he's up the wrong tree."

ANSAKI DEVOUT

Chapter Twenty-Four:
The Holy Inquisition

"So when will Alarico O'Donovan have his truth test, Juan?"

"He won't," replied the police chief, covering his mouth as he ate. They were sitting in a narrow alleyway, not far from the National Police barracks in Malaga. "You know, Pete, here at Casa Aranda, when I was a kid, the waiters were real gents. It was an honour to wear a long white jacket and serve the hot chocolate from a silver *cafetera* (kettle), from on high. The *churros* were light and feathery. It was so busy, it was one of the focal points of the city. The waiters were introducers, commission agents, message takers, and givers, and yet the service was impeccable."

"But at the press conference," insisted Pete, "you stated that there was to be a test."

"It was a ploy," said the policeman. "You see, I needed to get Moshe and his brother to come clean with me as to whatever they were hiding regarding Alarico. Think back, Pete, the brother, the Major. He spoke to us of tradition and an obligation and whether the Moshe had told us who he, Alarico, was. Then the Moshe realised and dashed in and carted the Major off, presumably to shut him up."

"And so you set up the press conference in collusion with them? To let Alarico off the hook?"

"Well said the policeman, it wasn't quite like that, but yes, in essence, they wanted Alarico's guilt or otherwise to be established based principally on a confession. It appeared that they believed that if he was allowed to declare, his innocence would be established. They were quite convinced that he would claim innocence"

"So you went along and organised the press conference in the Jordan hospital."

"As you well know, my friend, and later, and as a return favour, I had a meeting with them at which time they told me this extraordinary story.

"In the years around 1504 in Cordoba in Spain, the 'Abecasis' family was one of the many Sephardic Jewish families living in the Juderia (Jewish quarter). They were subjected to a pogrom organised by an inquisitor known as 'the Dark One' because of his excesses. An ancestor of Alarico's named Rodrigo instigated a rebellion of the nobles, freed the Jews, and personally helped the Abecasis family to escape. They say that he was hooded but that their ancestors recognized him. Well, the Abecasis family has kept in touch with the Medinachelis over the centuries. They were friendly with Alarico's mother and her family.

"So, when Alarico appeared on the scene as a doctor to work in Gaza, Moshe thought he had hit the jackpot. The original saviour was a Rodrigo de Medinacheli, and it is noted on records that when later questioned by agents of King Ferdinand he denied all knowledge. The family knew perfectly well what had happened, but he was adamant in denying it. It was put down at the time to being due to some mystical intervention. Throughout the history of this family, at crucial moments, it seems that some heroic figure has emerged, and always with the same story, total denial by the suspected author of the act. Recently in the world wars and on occasions long before, Medinachelis have emerged to save lives or carry out acts of heroism which they would later deny all knowledge of.

"A divine trait? Perhaps. Or a physiological flaw, who knows? Experts who were consulted have posed the possibility of disassociative identity disorder (DID), or multiple personality syndrome, although these are thought to be caused by trauma in early life rather than being genetically transmitted.

"But let's face it, psychology is hardly an exact science, being based on schools of thought, tendencies, and experimentation.

Well the story they told me was much longer and more detailed than I have recounted to you here, this in fact is just the salient skeleton of the story, Good grief did they go on? I needn't specify, I imagine, that Moshe and the Major are descendants of the Abecasis family?"

"Alarico has been tested privately by experts in the field of lie detection in the presence of a Notary Public and it has been televised. This has been done with our permission, and indeed our blessing, but we have not taken part in any way, as to do so would have been illegal, and our findings would have been judicially inconclusive."

"So we are back to where we started from," said Pete, "or rather you are."

"Not at all," replied Betardo with a big smile. "We have our assassin-come-crusader, but we can't get at him. If you think about it, there's not a shred of evidence to tie him to the murder. His lawyers would say that I just plucked him out of the air because I, with my unusual mindset, and based on escapades such as his striptease on the beach, decided that he was a likely suspect in our murder, all of which is true. As a matter of fact, he is now free, walking the streets, trying to escape from the press. He will probably laugh it all off, become a whiz at disguises, and escape, without leaving a trace, from the public eye, off to the mountains or into the sea. Oh, and don't forget that in all probability he has no idea that he is the killer. Yes, he has been told and he knows what is said, he reads it in the press, but he has no memory or conscious awareness of having committed the act."

"Yes," said Pete, "and in all reality, we do not know for certain that he was the killer. Only a certain police inspector knows, based on gut feel. And of course, Alarico defends what was done as he also now defends the justification for the act itself."

"But the case is not closed. We still need to establish exactly what happened and how," he said as he waved the waiter down. "The bill, please. We are leaving."

Pete smiled as the police chief led him on to a bus. People he must have known said hello, and Betardo smiled at them affably with various *"Buenos dias."*

"Buenos dias Jefe y compania," the driver cordially greeted them. *"A la Comisaria?"*

Betardo gave him a smile and a big thumbs up.

"Malaga's greatest beauty is its people, especially the normal people and the workers. I travel on public transport as often as I can so that I have contact with them. Whenever I have been to the hospitals, the atmosphere is wonderful, especially for the older folk, many of whom are generally suffering from one ailment or other. Here we are now," he added as the driver turned into a bus stop and opened the doors.

As they walked over the esplanade that surrounded the Comisaria Provincial de Policia, the National Police barracks, and Betardo's headquarters, they were greeted by a fully uniformed Guardia Civil captain, Jose Garcia. He saluted briskly and took Betardo by the arm in an aside.

"I am very sorry, Juan, that the weapon discovered was by mistake not shared with the task force."

"It's not a problem, Jose." Turning, he beckoned to Pete, who was standing discreetly to one side. "You know my friend Pete?"

"Yes of course, we shared the *Coin* adventure. By the way, Juan, I am so sorry that your suspect has been released. Obviously, you were mistaken."

Betardo did not reply, but just looked down as if in thought.

"Oh, and by the way, the report came through from Pakistan. I left it with Laura for you."

"And?" said Betardo.

"The fingerprints on the gun were not Sidi Hamou's, as we suspected they were." "So were they anybody's?"

"They belonged to Sidi Mohamed. The dead man, Sidi Hammou's father."

"So you have solved your case, Jose. Your victim was assassinated by a deceased killer – incredibly, the suspect's father."

"Our case, Juan. Tell me, then, that our O'Donovan suspect is then completely off the hook?"

"Don't worry, Jose. I will make sure you receive a copy of my final report once it has gone to Madrid."

With that, he turned on his heel and continued toward the Comisaria with Pete in tow.

They sat on the raised dais in the exposition theatre of the Police building. The hall was empty except for Betardo, Pete, Chief Inspector Laura Galvez the criminologist, and the typist.

"Laura, you are great to work with and I am a disaster. I want to apologise."

"No, Juan. I know who and how you are. I weighed you up a long time ago and, well, let's just say you are an unusual policeman. But you are a good man with no malice, which is unheard of in someone of your rank and stature. You are also the best detective in Spain."

Betardo blushed gracefully and grunted something. She continued, "Your friend Captain Garcia came by with a piece of undisclosed evidence, the murder weapon. You do know about it then? What is this man's problem?"

"Please, Laura, from this moment on keep him out of the case. It's our investigation and once we are in place I will make a report with our findings directly to Madrid. It will be our joint report, Laura."

"That's generous of you Juan, but not necessary. You have my loyalty anyway."

"I know that. Two things, Laura. You know Pete, my old friend? He will be an interested observer of our work. Is that OK with you?"

Pete gave her a thumbs-up and a wink. She smiled and bowed her head slightly in acceptance. "Of course, Chief Inspector."

"And Laura, please get one of your people to liaise with the Fuengirola branch. The five suspects from there, the Rif lads and the two from the Atlas, you know they were on the bike concentration list. Find out where they hang out. These sorts of lads always have a favourite joint, bar, or something. If it could be now, wonderful. Close to the chest please, hush hush."

"I'll get my best sergeant on to it now. Anything else, Chief? You know, you can have your own people who will do your bidding."

"No, no spare me," said Betardo in an imploring tone. "I am a good. What was it that man called me, a nice man with a strange stammer? I know, sleuth, he called me a sleuth. Sherlock Holmes was a sleuth, Poirot. I like to be a sleuth, I prefer not to handle staff – I am simply disastrous at it."

"The Pink Panther," said Pete.

"You see what I mean, Laura? Even my friends." They all laughed, even the efficient typist.

An attractive uniformed woman came in and saluted. She sat with Laura and they talked rapidly to each other. After a few minutes, she left.

"And now, said Betardo, I'm going to ask you all to bear with me as I go over a few bits, out loud, as my memory is a bit limited and I will need your help."

"When Captain Garcia briefed us on Sidi Hamou, in fact on the whole affair, it stuck in my mind that he mentioned Marrakech and the Madrasah, twice in fact. Both the father and the son attended. Now none of you here present were with us, but when Captain Garcia and I visited the home of Alarico's girlfriend, the Diez girl, her father – that's the nice fellow, the one who called me sleuth. In fact, he called us both sleuths, but I'm sure he meant me," he chuckled, "not Garcia. Garcia's more of a plod." He chuckled again. "Sorry, just venting my irritation here. Well, he told us that the girl went to Marrakech to study Sufism for a spell, and that was the first time, and now with Garcia's narrative, it's mentioned twice more? One must acknowledge that

Garcia always raises the hare but then fails to see it, never mind take a shot at it."

"You mean that as a top sleuth, you don't like coincidences?" put in Pete.

"Well, it is something to think about," said Laura. Let's have a crisp history of all that happened with our suspects. Would you like us to contact the DST in Marrakech again? They were very helpful. I'll get dates on all the history we have Mohamed and Hamou, father and son. Travel dates, study dates, all they've got."

A voice from the entrance requested permission to come in.

"It's your Sergeant, Laura. That was quick. Sit down with us and tell us, Sergeant," said Betardo pleasantly. "What goodies have you got for us?"

The young woman approached, saluted, and looked at Chief Inspector Galvez for confirmation.

"Yes of course, Sergeant. Please do relax and talk to us. Our only interest here is the job at hand."

"Well Ma'am, Sir, an Inspector at Fuengirola was involved in locating the five at the start of the investigation, as they appeared on the videos we had of the concentration. As he is often involved in the street drags they do as a team for pickpockets and the like, he was able to identify four of them as hanging out at a particular bar. The fifth he never made contact with – there is a search warrant out for him. Well, the owner of the bar is a friendly Rif guy named Aksil.

If you want, the inspector can go there and ask any questions."

"No, Sergeant," said Betardo. "What we need is for you to line up a small team of big Nacionales, tough-looking guys, drive to Fuengirola in a big scary police van, and bring them in.

"Who?" asked the sergeant.

"Aksil and the four suspects of course. If they are not there, find them. If Aksil objects, just tell him to close the bar. Ask them to come in for questioning. If they disagree arrest them on suspicion of loitering or possession or whatever you can think up. You request the assistance of the Fuengirola branch so that no one escapes, not one of the four, and to locate them if they are not there."

"You want me to run this, Chief?" she said, worriedly looking from one officer to the other.

"You could do with the experience, Sergeant," said Galvez, looking at Betardo with a resigned face.

"But I'm from Madrid, Ma'am. I've never been to Fuengirola."

"So much the better," said Betardo. "Think of it – task force sergeant from Madrid, making all the local *policias* nervous. Now what's your name, Sergeant?"

"Perez, Sir. Maria Perez."

"Well, do it, Perez. Your orders are from the top, the very top. Take no ifs or buts – this is in the interests of national security. Oh, and keep the prisoners, guests, together in a room with a guard when they get here. I want them worried."

"Talk about the deep end," Pete remarked as she left, saluting and standing to attention.

"A little power. I just hope she doesn't have to be restrained from beating up the prisoners," replied Betardo.

"Fun in your work," retorted Galvez somewhat drily.

"Yes, for me, sure, and also for her, for Maria. Why not? Stops the staleness setting in."

Chapter Twenty-Five :
Interrogation

"Watch him and listen carefully, he's very good. Speaks very quietly, though. You need to concentrate. Probably does it on purpose. This is interrogation Cell One, for the record," she said with a grin.

Pete sat quietly with Laura, waiting for the interrogation to begin in the next cell, which they could view through their one-way, soundproofed screen. The sound came to them from the mikes installed for recording the sessions.

The door of the adjoining cell was pushed open and the prisoner was guided in. He looked bemused and unhappy, shaking his head as if to clear a haze.

"Advise him of his rights, and of his right to keep silent. Check the mikes and equipment. I want this recorded properly," said Betardo quietly. Then he sat down to face the prisoner.

"You're the bar owner?" asked Betardo. "Aksil Dasulafi?"
"Yes, Sir. You asked for me, so you know who I am."

"Are you homosexual?"

"No, I am not. Why do you ask that?"

"It may be a non-relevant question just thrown in at random," whispered Laura in Pete's ear, " In spite of the soundproofed screen, or may well be a leading question based on Juan's theories. Which are often quite wild," she added, chuckling under her breath.

"Do you understand what the charges are?" said Betardo, suddenly speaking loudly and surprisedly, as if addressing a child.

"What charges?" Aksil asked, raising his voice in indignation. "I have done nothing."

"Well, in that case, in a short while, you will leave here with our thanks. If applied, the charges would be conspiracy to murder a foreign diplomat and terrorism, which carry a prison sentence of twenty-five to fifty years on either count. Of course, they may be commuted to permanent revisable imprisonment."

"But what are you saying? I just run a bar. I think I should have a lawyer. This is crazy."

"That would be the rest of your life. How old are you? Yes, thirty-six. Two lifetimes in fact. But of course, Aksil, you may have a lawyer, right away in fact. Shall I organise it for you?"

"Well, what do you think, Sir?" said Aksil. "I think," he said cockily, "that you are playing me along."

"Possibly. On the other hand, of course, there is the fact that the men, coincidentally of your race and frequent visitors to your establishment, came straight to you after murdering the Senator at Sotogrande."

248

"No, no, no they are just kids, they always come to me to drink tea. I talk to them and mess around. They just went on a spree, a day on the beach at Sotogrande."

"A killing spree? They went on a killing spree and then they came back to report in. Five men went. Yet we have only four and yourself in custody. Where are you hiding the fifth? I have squads waiting on my word to raid your home and that of your parents."

Aksil put his face into his hands, his cockiness evaporating. He had visions of the police searching his home, his wife's face, the crying kids, the inevitable "Aksil, what have you done?"

"Why do you think this? What have I done?"

"Well," said Betardo in a low voice that the other man was straining to hear. "There are two things here. There's what you did do and what you could have done. You are married, I am told, children. Your parents, immigrants, well settled and prosperous."

"What do you want? Tell me what you want."

"Tell me about Mohamed, Hamou to begin with. Everything you know."

"Hamou?" Aksil sounded surprised. "He is quiet, friendly, from Atlas mountains, a real Berber, and big. He keeps himself to himself. No! There was one day, one day a guy got very nasty at the bar, swearing, and there were girls. Hamou was sitting at a table drinking tea. Without standing, he took the guy, and he was big, the drunk, by the neck and leaned him over so he could whisper in his ear. And we were all surprised as the guy just turned and left the bar without another word. I know he was strong, but why do you not ask Simu about him? They were mates."

"We already spoke to Simu, and in fact to all of them. We are after the less obvious bits and believe me, we never give up."

"So all of this has been staged for my benefit? If you have already interviewed the lads?"

"Tell me more about Hamou. Who was he with? We know Simu was just his assistant, his runner. An ex-convict, also from the High Mountains, whom he took pity on apparently."

"Oh, I know!" Aksil burst out in an apparent effort to provide something useful. "You know, Inspector, how when you work with people, like in a bar or something, you get to notice things, little things that most people don't see. Well, there was something between Hamou and that Afra, you know, one of the lads, the very young one. The way they did not look at each other or speak much. It was strange."

"The young one, the one who saw the shooting of the Senator?"

"Well, he says he did. I think he did because he got all emotional. He was crying," "OK, let's have him in. Let's talk to him."

"What, with me in here?"

"Yes, of course with you here. You may embarrass each other, but as long as we find out all that's going on I don't care. You need to see yourself as being secretly on my side. After all, we are, are we not? Sergeant," he said, raising his voice "Please bring in the boy Afra. He's the young kid amongst the prisoners – visitors, I should say."

The boy was guided into the cell. He was visibly shaking.

"Why is this young man so nervous?" Betardo asked the sergeant, who just shrugged. "Perhaps he's guilty, Sir,"

"No, no way, he doesn't look the type. Bring him some orange juice or something, Sergeant."

"Your name is a good Berber name, very ancient and noble – Afra. Afra, we just want to understand many things, so I thought you could help us. That's all we want – a little help. Is that OK?"

The boy squirmed as he sat there, unable to be comforted, to relax. "When did you start selling dope, boy?"

"But I don't," he protested whiningly. "I hate drugs, and my mother would kill me. Who's telling you these things?"

He glared at Aksil. "And what about your father? Does he approve of what you do?"

"I don't have a father."

"So, let me see. You live with your mother. Is that it, and you have a job?"

"No. I was studying but I left it."

"Later he was training as a hairdresser," put in Aksil.

251

"But he left it as well, I imagine?" said Betardo. "So your mother feeds you and houses you, but what do you do for money, Afra? Look, you wear Nike and Superdry. And please tell me, when did you two meet? Was it when Aksil persuaded you to leave the hairdresser?"

Both men were silent. Then Aksil spoke hesitatingly: "In the bar."

"And Hamou, did you meet Hamou in the bar? I'm speaking to you, Afra," he said, as the young man seemed to have sunk into a stupor born of fear or lack of sleep.

"Yes, Sir," stuttered Afra. "Is he your friend?" "Yes, Sir."

"And is Aksil your friend?" The inspector banged the table. "Aksil, is he your friend?"

"No, Sir, he was. I thought he was," stuttered the nineteen-year-old, starting to tremble again.

"So what was he if not your friend? Tell me what he was to you. Was he the head of your band of terrorist killers?"

The other man, the bar owner, kept trying to speak, and Betardo aggressively waved him to silence.

"Tell me what he was to you, or you will be charged with murder." "He did things to me," said Afra, not looking up at the other man. "Things?" asked Betardo quietly. "What things?"

"Things like a man would do to a girl." The young guy was weeping now. "You mean he became your homosexual lover?"

"He wouldn't give me any money so he gave me to Hamou. He was such a bastard." "So Mohamed gave money to Aksil for you, to buy you?"

"No, Hamou was good to me, he just paid Aksil to leave me alone. Then Aksil was jealous. I was happy with Hamou. But my mother, this will break her heart. In Islam, this does not happen."

"Yes, it happens, Afra, just there are different customs and laws in the West. You have been brought up in Spain and have been told by your parents how things are in Morocco, but times have changed. Now tell me about Hamou. Was he a good lover, passionate?"

"No, I don't want to talk about that."

"Do you want us to call your mother now, have her sit on the other side of that screen and listen?"

"No, please, it would kill her. She's such a good woman, and since my father died there's only me to look after her.

"He liked to hold me, sleep with me, Hamou. He would make love to me, not like Aksil. Aksil treated me like a dog. Mohamed would be gentle. Then, one night he was asleep. I was up against him. He began to get very hard and then with no warning he penetrated me. It hurt me with no lubricant, but he was so excited and asleep that he was very different, and he kept calling me 'Sally Anne, Sally Anne.' I don't know who that was, but…"

"Stop. Stop right there. Sergeant," Betardo raised his voice, "this interview is terminated." As the sergeant came bustling in, he spoke loudly, as much for her benefit as for the recording.

"This is Chief Inspector Juan Betardo of the Judicial Police. This interview is hereby terminated. The two interviewees will be held incommunicado by the provincial Judicial Police under the command of Chief Inspector Galvez until my further orders. Neither prisoner will be charged at all as long as they cooperate fully. Furthermore, the recordings of this interview are to be removed at this moment and handed to CI Laura Galvez for safekeeping in her safe.

"Do you understand?" he asked the men. "You will not be charged with anything as long as you cooperate by remaining willingly in this Police Comisaria for as long as I say. Maybe a few hours, maybe a day or two. Everything that has happened here in this room will be a secret and will never be known. And you, Aksil, will keep Afra's secret and help him as a brother. If I hear otherwise I will close your business."

"Are you really the Chief Inspector?" asked Aksil.

"Yes I am, and you'd better tremble in your shoes if ever you see my face again. You lied to me about being homosexual right from the start. You also led me to the boy, knowing that the facts about you would emerge, so evidently you have bigger items to hide. If I hear you mentioned in a case ever again, I will go for you and ruin you."

The bar owner just stood there abjectly, his face a picture of misery and fear. The boy just cried, his face in his hands. Betardo put an arm around him and ruffled his hair.

"Come on, it's all over now. The sergeant will send for some nice sandwiches and hot coffee for you. And Sergeant, please get them a TV to watch."

ANSAKI DEVOUT

Chapter Twenty-Six:
Sidi Hamou

"Laura, please get your people to call Spanish Military Intelligence, ask for Aparicio, ask him to get round here at once, tell him we have news. Also please get me the commander of our GEO, Police Tactical Unit. I am not sure if I need to speak first to the superintendent who runs the whole outfit. No, I know, get me a fellow named Inspector Ofarra. I know him from before he went into the GEO. Miguel Ofarra runs the 40 and 50 operative groups who train in this area."

"40 and 50?" queried Laura.

"Yes, that's what they call them. Let's meet in say thirty minutes, with our colleagues from GEO and Intelligence here in the hall."

They were sitting in their usual spot, Betardo, Pete, Laura, and the secretary-come- computer-operator Agatha.

"Do you realise Juan, that we air condition the whole hall just for our little meetings?"

"Laura, step outside the building and climb onto the roof. You will see that we generate enough solar electricity to power half of Malaga," he laughed. "Anyway, we've cracked the case, so we deserve a bit of comfort."

"Yes, what was all that bit of Betardo dramatics about?" Pete briefly aped Betardo's last words in the interrogation facility. "This Interrogation is now over, totally over, secrecy is essential must all be secretive, mum on the subject."

Betardo held up a hand, a wide grin splitting his face.

"Heavens, did it sound that bad? I just wanted to get the kid off the hook. Not a bad lad. Fell foul of that Aksil and his devious ways. To be frank it was his mother I was thinking of, stupid as it may sound."

"So who's Sally Anne, Juan?"

"Well, Laura and I more or less know. She's the Diez girl, Alarico's friend."

"Sally Anne, Afra's Sally Anne, Hamou's Sally Anne, the one he thinks he's making love to in his sleep. Well, it could be any one of the millions of Sally Annes that exist in the world.

"Think of it now" went on Betardo, "Sally Anne Diez at seventeen, stunningly beautiful, in love with justice and fair play and reading philosophy, Santa Teresa of God, Hinduism, and seeking Brahmacharya and Sufism to reach Haquiqa and Marifa, the ultimate levels of mysticism and truth."

"Well, she gets on a plane and sets off to Marrakech to pursue Sufism. She finds a school as close to the Grand Madrasah as she can get. Probably stays in a small Arab hotel or whatever, and walks around wearing her modest *djellaba* and a hijab. But it being a special moment for her, a time of extreme devotion, and probably also so as not to be spotted as a foreigner, she draws the headscarf around to partially cover her face. The general effect is that she stands out like a sore thumb, and although they respect her modesty, people in Morocco are naturally curious. Stares follow her wherever she goes, despite her total oblivion to the attention she is getting.

"So one day a group of boys follow her. They block her way and shout at her, and she tries unsuccessfully to calm them in her poor Darija (the oral tongue spoken in the Maghreb). There is a young man who has observed her each day and made a point of passing on the same street as her. He sees what is happening from the other side of the street and crosses. He is dressed as do the Ulama (Islamic students), humbly attired in the *thawb* (body cover) and *keffiyah*, turban on his head. He is tall, and as he draws nearer it is evident that he is powerfully built. He speaks quietly and the boys stop shouting. They converse briefly. Then one of the boys bends down and kisses the hem of his *thawb*. He, the Ulama, is embarrassed, or so she thinks. He waves them away, laughing, playing it down, evidently for her benefit. They go, but they are not laughing – they are shouting *Allahu Akhbar* (God is great) as they go. She is mystified. He explains as he hastens her away from the spot as people are looking, that they, the boys, agreed to behave, and so they became friends. He does not tell her that one of the boys is from the high mountains and that he has recognized him as the son of Sidi Mohamed who fights in Afghanistan for Allah.

"He tells her he is Hamou, and as the days go by he introduces her to Djema'a el -Fna, the heart of the city, and its amazing hustle and bustle. Wherever they go there are always people who greet him and kiss his hem, his hand, or even his shoulder."

"That's a hell of a fiction to base criminal suspicion on, especially from a top scientific police sleuth," laughed Pete.

"You just wait, Russian. Let's just see how close to the mark I get."

"We have yeahs from both Aparicio and Ofarra for a Zoom conference in say ten minutes." "Fine, go for it, Laura. Top security – they must be alone."

The big screen flickers and the three participants in the electronic conference appear in separate boxes.

"Aparicio, Miguel, good afternoon, and thanks for appearing so promptly," leads Betardo. "Hello, Chief Inspector. Miguel Ofarra here. Nice to see you, Juan. So long a time."

"Hello, Juan, Aparicio here. I am all ears, secure line. I hope it's good. We need a break."

"Hi you both, here it is then. My team of sleuths and I here gathered, have finally come up with a highly probable link between the Spanish doctor suspected of the murder of the Senator, and the reputedly deceased Arab terrorist known as Sidi Mohamed through his son, the wraithlike operator known as Sidi Hamou. You are aware, Miguel, I trust, that the deceased Sidi Mohamed's fingerprints have been confirmed as those on the gun that assassinated the colonel from the ME Democracy only recently, and yet he, Sidi Mohamed, died at the fortress in Pakistan all those years ago, or so we were told."

"Hence the urgency," said Ofarra.

"Hence the urgency indeed," replied Betardo. "Now before I go any further I will make it clear that you guys will make no contact whatsoever with the suspect. This person will be my territory and domain as I need to go further in establishing the ins and outs of the case. You gentlemen can use the name I am about to give you as the focal address for an intense control to be set up to detain Sidi Hamou. Our own police operations squad here raided the same address and area just a few days ago, so they can furnish everything, maps, info the works. I just thought that between the two of you and your people, you should be able to seal off the area.

"Oh sorry, Miguel. This is Aparicio..." said Betardo as an afterthought "Coronel," interrupted Aparicio. "Military Intelligence."

"Hello Coronel, I am Inspector Ofarra, GEO. I will need to speak to my superintendent, but coming from Juan's level we can start to do our homework immediately. And of course, I will be delighted to cooperate with you and your team, Coronel. Once I have permission we will be en route immediately, studying the info and maps as we go."

"Fine," agreed Aparicio with a nod. "My agents and I will be there imminently we will decide on a suitable centre of operation as we go, and will keep you advised, Inspector."

"Ok," said Betardo. "I can give you one hour and no more to seal the area. On the hour exactly I will be knocking on the door of the house in question to interview the suspect and indeed her family. No disturbances, please. The chances are that the young lady of the house is the lover of many years ago, and perhaps today, of Sidi Hamou."

"That is one hell of a break, Juan. If it pans out, there is of course a very high likelihood that our man is hiding out in the house or immediate area."

"Well, I doubt that," said Juan, "but we do now for the first time have a connection to the wraith. Before this, people were even doubting his very existence."

As the Zoom screens shut down, Pete drily commented, "Seems that we have the scene set and prepared for our showdown with the archvillain. Gets more like an Edmund Campion finale at every step."

"A parody of a parody? Perhaps," retorted the beaming detective. "I never knew you read English books. Always had you down as a Dostoyevsky and Tolstoy fan, with a smattering of Maxim Gorky thrown in kowtowing to the Reds, although you do have the name wrong

– it's Albert Campion you're referring to, unless, of course, you're talking about the saint."

"My, you are very unaware of Russia. The ties with Great Britain went back years and we read your authors avidly, at least until things got difficult. But hold on a minute, you're Spanish."

"And very able, may I say, to line up intelligence and the Geo's to protect the scene, just in case the hare is there and lifted," put in Laura Galvez, clapping her hands.

"You mean raising the hare, as in *D'ye Ken John Peel*," replied Betardo, starting to sing the opening lines of the popular hunting ditty.

"You must understand, Pete, that our civil war created a time gap in Spanish literature which we have ably redressed in the present. Historically though, Spanish literature is rich and varied. And after all, we do have Don Quijote.

"I really must comment," said Laura Galvez, "that we do seem to be in a very frivolous mindset, given that we are dealing with murderers, with killers, and it is you, Chief Inspector, who's setting the tone."

There was an embarrassed silence.

"Yes, you are right, Laura, I do set the tone, and Pete understands why."

"There is no evil here," said the big Russian. These are children who are dreaming of a better world, who have an inkling of what evil is, and who want it to stop one day. Children who each in their way believe the Our Father when it says, 'Thy Kingdom come, thy will be done on Earth as it is in Heaven'. Children who believe that the triumph of good over evil is possible. I have seen evil, touched it, and even been a part of it. I have seen such things, such soul-destroying badness, that you do not want to know as it would spoil your life."

"But I, Laura, am a policeman," cut in Betardo. "I respect the rule of law as few do in the world of today, but nobody can ask me to be unhappy, especially if I see some light, unusual light, perhaps even godsent, at the end of a very dark tunnel. I ask you one thing, Laura, and also this young girl who has sat with us all these days, patiently and with great reserve and class, and has heard everything. Agatha," he said, and she smiled shyly at them. "We will go now to the house of these people who are crucial to understanding what the case is all about, and you can sit outside in a radio van and hear it all. I will get the tech people to set it up right now, and then *vamonos*."

Chapter Twenty-Seven: The Virgen

At exactly four pm Juan Betardo and Pete arrived at the front gates of the Diez house in Entrerrios to be welcomed by the small aggressive *bodeguera*-style dog and the larger *dogo*. The *dogo* barked and wagged its tail, but the small one seemed to mean business, leaping up at the gates aggressively.

"The small one is named Miss Victoria and dislikes Guardia Civiles, we were told. She may even have a point," he smiled.

"Getting bitchy are we now?" teased Pete.

Then the woman came marching down the drive. "Maria, this is Maria. Doesn't like police. Or us? "What do you want?" she shouted as she came.

"Good afternoon, Maria. You remember me? From the National Police?" "What do you want? The Señor is not home."

Well, the Señora, or the young lady Sally Anne." She spoke into an intercom.

"She is saying that I am here from the police, and accompanied by a criminal."

He looked at Pete with a blank expression masking his amusement. The big man looked back at him and said nothing.

265

Sally Anne and Alarico came down to the gate. He looked weak and walked slowly with an old person's gait, and she supported him with her arm.

"Hello Inspector, sorry, Chief Inspector." He put his hand out through the gate and they shook hands. "And Pete. From our heady Israel days," he said.

"How are you?" said Pete. "This kind of wound takes a long time to heal."

"I am exceptionally fit," replied Alarico. "All this running over mountains and hills for so many years, so for this reason the doctors tell me that my recovery will be much faster."

"Yes," said Juan, "but only rest heals. You must rest."

She just looked on. Both men summing her up and she them. She was sultry, and stunningly beautiful in her casual hair and clothes. The two men, both hardened in their fields and having met many such girls in their time, were trying to affix a label to begin to get a grip on the individual, and failing.

"I suppose you've come for tea," she smiled, and they were both beguiled. "Yes," she said, "the decent copper, the policeman with a soul. And," she giggled, "and the criminal. You must forgive Maria, it's just that you are so big and foreign and, well, you do look, experienced." She giggled some more.

"Hello, Sally Anne," said Betardo, bowing slightly from the waist. "Pete and Juan at your service. May we come in, please?"

"What is it that you want exactly?" asked the girl. "Tea," said Betardo.

She smiled. "Hoisted by my own device, I suppose."

"And a friendly chat. You must be aware that a friendly chat with me will always be preferable to alternatives potentially engendered by your own, resumé, should I say."

"You are very cryptic, Chief Inspector, and have me at a total disadvantage." Alarico opened the garden door and the two men entered.

"Come on, Sally Anne, it's just them, and Pete's not even a copper."

"What about that bloody great van they've come in? Probably got an army in there." Pete and Betardo looked at each other and chuckled.

They sat on an outside porch that surrounded the house, from where the views of the nearby Mijas Mountain range, tinged with an unusual purple and enshrouded in a light mist, gave the impression of something African.

"An uncanny resemblance to some view from Marrakech of the mountains," said Betardo. "So I've been told," replied Alarico. "Not been there myself," he said, "but Sally Anne."

"Yes," said Betardo. "So I was told on my last visit here by, I believe it was by Mr Diez, and the story about her pursuit of higher things, and of her travel to study Sufism."

Nobody said anything, so Betardo continued. "I didn't know her then, at all, yet had this vision rush into my head of a lovely young girl, totally covered up in the Islamic fashion, attempting to blend into the cosmopolitan Marrakech atmosphere and attracting the wrong attention. And of a gallant and strapping young man stepping into the fray. But he is a killer, a multiple assassin, and wanted all over the world, and you are harbouring a runaway, an undesirable."

"Sidi Hamou, Mohamed Al Tac Farinal, is my husband," she said quietly. "We were married in the High Mountains when I was seventeen. So you see, Chief Inspector, your theories are all out. I met him in Chellah in the ancient resting place of the Al Merinid kings close to Rabat, and we were kindred spirits and we spoke for hours and days. He is no murderer, he is a defender of children, all children. He has seen terrible things being done to children, rape, humiliation, torture. He has seen the results of famine and gratuitous war. He is fighting the many initiatives being embarked upon by evil people to alter the genetic and social reality of the child. The world is in a bad place today, and people like my husband are its hope."

"I regret to inform you then," said Betardo, "that your husband Sidi Hamou will soon be under arrest."

"Chief Inspector, Alarico speaks well of you, but let me assure you that you and your kind do not even begin to comprehend what and whom you are dealing with. Hamou is as a spirit, he does not exist for me or for you; his presence or being as a person or in a place is purely transient. We had our short time of happiness, after which we went in our separate ways."

"So you never see him?" asked Betardo.

"You will never see him, Chief Inspector. For you, he does not exist, and for me, the few and fleeting nights of passion and intense love we have shared are enough for a lifetime, knowing what he stands for and represents for a growing number of his faithful in so many countries.

"The important thing for me as a bystander is that slowly it becomes patent to all of those abusing power in one way or another, that to do so may well lead to their termination as human beings. And yes, Inspector, it is happening all over the world."

"You are referring of course to those known as Ansaki?" asked Betardo. "I was unaware that they were related to the Al Tac Farinal family's activities."

"I don't know that they are, Chief Inspector. Perhaps these things are just spontaneous happenings, the world physical and the human race trying to breathe?"

"And by what right do you set yourself up to be an approver of such acts?" asked the policeman.

There was a clatter as the teacups and pots were set on the tables.

"Answer him, or I will," sounded the strident voice of Mrs Diez, who had come in with Maria and the tea things.

"I will, Mother, I will, at the right moment. Just let the man ask his questions. It seems that he could potentially care. You see, Inspector, the adage of who polices the policeman is always raised to defend the existing democratic system, which does not work."

"It's the best we've got so far."

"The best, Chief Inspector, given its record of killings, cheating, and just about everything else. Think of it: you start a democratic organisation, a trade union, a political party, or a religion, and with time the more ambitious members begin to work all out to get on top of their fellows. The final scenario is that the collective becomes evil in one way or another, although we the public are sold on it being what it originally was. Only the individual can be pure.

"That's one hell of an assertion," said Juan.

"And it's in the nick of time. I read a book about Somalia by a man named Gerald Hanley. He spoke about old men in every country with complete memories of their cultures in their heads. How they are despised in favour of the worship of money, technology, and war. And how a few generations later their descendants are searching for evidence, curios which would give ideas of how they had once lived. Seeking clues of how the Red Indians lived before the brash USA stamped them out. Meanwhile, they are going into space to carry their lust for finding new people to dominate, control, and order about, all in a sick pursuit of creating consumers for consumer goods. Now all this insane hamster treadwheel that we are on is kept oiled by a certain type of person. But the question arises, as ostensibly we do have our built-in checks and balances, are they, these people who oil the wheel corrupt? And the answer is invariably yes.

"Well, my answer is that the world must be rid of such people."

"And I will again ask you," said Betardo as he held up a bone china teacup to see the Chinese lady at the bottom of the cup, "Why you?"

"I have given up my son, my baby son. I have never even seen him, or can ever know him or of him, or him me, or of me. Silent tears fell down her cheeks slowly and dropped to the clay-tiled floor. One day he will be told who his parents were, his father and grandfather, and his heartbroken mother, and his chest will swell with pride. He will continue the tradition of purification, and many will walk the same road. I know now though, how Mary felt when they took her son from her.

"My mother wants me to try to find him and reclaim him, as she says it's tearing me apart. She doesn't know, not really, that what is destroying me is what goes on in the world. I try to set myself apart from it and lead a young, flippant life, and it works, most of the time. But then it comes back when I hear of what a group of people is doing to the less fortunate collective in whatever part of the world, and realise that it's the same bunch of evil moronic politicians, billionaires, powermongers, or their friends or copycats. You know my only solace in such moments is the thought that a movement or set of movements, an unstoppable process has started which could, for the first time in history, make a real difference.

"So who am I to approve of the multiple killings of so many evil, corrupt, and undesirable persons all over the world? I am a suffering mother, like the millions of suffering mothers whose children have been dragged off, shot, murdered, tortured, or are under threat from the zombified forces of these evil movers of affairs in so many parts of our globe."

"And who knows about you and Sidi Hamou and the child?"

"They know everything, Chief Inspector," said Mrs Diez in her strident tones. "Now, of course, since I began making enquiries for the child, who is no longer a child, the cat is totally out of the bag. Spanish Intelligence has had our house under surveillance for years now, presumably since my son-in-law," she spoke sarcastically, "became prominent in the world of terminating child murderers."

"Yes, Juan," cut in the girl, "they know everything. They control everything, everywhere. You and I, you may well have come here today labouring under the misapprehension that the link between Hamou and I was a secret, but they have long been aware of us, of me. What they cannot achieve is any way to run down Sidi Hamou, and as to his father Sidi Mohamed, we heard that he was being held responsible for the second assassination and that his prints had been discovered on the murder weapon. Not bad for a man long dead. There is a huge buildup in the Arab world, of expectation surrounding these two heroes and their undisclosed heir. And of course, world intelligence services can do nothing about the emergence of new Ansaki all the time and everywhere."

Made in the USA
Las Vegas, NV
22 July 2024

92552256R00154